Tl

To Janice —
With very best wishes!

Tru-1
1998

Thank you for sharing
Al Jr. with me!

The Clay Pigeon

Trude Knapp-Drinkwater

VANTAGE PRESS
New York

This book is a work of fiction, and substituted persons of the author's choosing are included. Names of characters were chosen from the ranks of acquaintances or simply made up, and are not intended to represent any real person. Any similarity to real persons, living or dead, is purely coincidental.

FIRST EDITION

All rights reserved, including the right of
reproduction in whole or in part in any form.

Copyright © 1998 by Trude Knapp-Drinkwater

Published by Vantage Press, Inc.
516 West 34th Street, New York, New York 10001

Manufactured in the United States of America
ISBN: 0-533-12442-5

Library of Congress Catalog Card No.: 97-90606

0 9 8 7 6 5 4 3 2 1

To Crestina and Michyal, a deep debt of gratitude

Prologue

Silence exploded! Cassandra's peace and serenity were demolished, shattered like a sledge hammer through an expanse of plate glass—all terminated like the creeping cracks in a windshield. The persistent, invading, and repetitious peal of the phone was particularly annoying because she had just replaced the ringer with a melody, but this time it came through the quiet with a jolting surge, a sense of urgency to the tone. Should she let her home be invaded? Her home to her was what Tara had been to Scarlett—her only constant in a turbulent world. When seemingly rejected by everyone, it was always her haven. It never disappointed her, either. It was just there. It wove a web around her, making her feel that the world was okay, even when it wasn't. It offered her private places where she could dream, a substitute for which she craved.

Hating her weakness of giving in to another electronic gadget, she warily picked it up. Why hadn't she let the answering machine accept the interruption!? Too late now. She was committed.

Cass had made the biggest commitment of her life many years ago on that very date, the fourth of December. It seemed that her thirty-two years of marriage had commenced eons ago. Having been alone for nearly twenty years, that anniversary had been put to rest—until that shocking telephone call.

The voice of her ex-sister-in-law was not strange to Cass, as they had been friends for many years and had always kept in touch, all throughout the trauma and heartbreak of Cass's divorce. Peg was in the Tropics, while Cass was still in the northern climes. She had tossed around the idea of going south to get a head start on her tan, but cross-country skiing and sled-dog racing had kept her home to date.

Due to her excitement, Peg's voice was much higher pitched than usual, but her New York accent still came through.

"Cass, you are not going to believe this, but as God is my judge, it is no ploy. As of today, you are twenty-five thousand dollars richer!"

"That sounds great, but how did I manage that?"

"Cass, I've known this for many years. It is a treasury bond which just matured with your name as beneficiary if alive at this time. Rex left it with directions to forward it to you." Dead, blatant silence. "He did love you, Cass, and knew long before he died that cheating on you was the biggest mistake of his life. God, how we do miss him. He is up there, Cass, and we know, as we are certain that you do, how often he has smiled when looking down upon his government plaque, supported by a sleek but well-endowed mermaid. No one else arranged for any kind of memorial, but everyone knows that you did. Somehow, Rex also knows that his U. S. Government issued American flag is still flying over his favorite maritime museum."

Always a practical thinker, but stunned to the point of being nearly speechless, Cass recovered.

"What were your directions had I not survived?" she asked.

"Certainly not that bitch sister of yours. He hated her greedy, conniving guts to the day he died. It is clearly designated to go to The American Cancer Society."

"Please send it by insured mail, Peg. This is a megashocker, but strangely enough, I already know where the major part of that will be invested—Rex's favorite vacation locale."

"Holy mackerel, Alaska?"

"That's affirmative, Peg, but it's salmon up there, not mackerel."

"You won't trek up there alone, will you, Cass?"

"I can't imagine sharing a secret, treasured rendezvous like that with anyone else, Peg, and I know the exact place to go. I promise to keep you informed and thank you for being my trusted and loyal friend for all these years. This will be a definite upgrade in the game of my roller-coaster life, economically, physically, emotionally, and spiritually."

That whole conversation seemed to drown Cass in fond, heart-wrenching memories. She mentally wandered back to the foot of Mt. McKinley in their luxurious Pace Arrow motor home, The Soonerville Trolley. Rex loved his constant companion, a lovable, loyal black cocker spaniel named Sooner, for whom he had named the land yacht. For two months, Rex had been so relaxed, happy, and contented in Alaska, his first extended vacation after retiring from thirty-one years of government service. He loved the slow pace of outdoor living. Yes, that was the location to leave another permanent memorial to Rex.

From Alaska, Cass's mind wandered to Key West, Florida, where they had spent some other memorable months while he was a United States naval officer. The U.S.S. *Bernadou*, a destroyer, was tied up for repairs, and its chief engineer, Rex, still had to spend some nights aboard as duty officer. On one dreamlike, calm, and still night, he asked the steward to take two wardroom chairs up on the deck. While sitting there, quietly sipping coffee, it was eerie to observe a submarine, sleekly, and oh, so furtively, gliding by them on its way out to sea. They knew some of those boys, so held hands firmly while uttering a silent prayer for their safe return.

Those were uncertain days, with World War Two still raging, but they did not lack for humorous instances. Their favorite was the time when three destroyers were tied up side by side. They were still in Key West, where President Harry Truman had his winter White House, but it had no swimming pool, so he appeared at the officer's club pool now and then. Cass was always thrilled to see him there with all his Secret Service men. It was one of those days that, again, Rex had the duty and asked the executive officer to go to the pool and escort Cass back aboard for dinner.

In order to board the Bernadou, one had to cross the decks of two other destroyers. They all looked alike to Cass. It seemed strange to her that most of the officers in the wardroom were from one of the sister ships. Before the first course was served, Rex suddenly appeared with his inimitable grin and declared, "Okay, Howie, nice try! You are on the wrong ship, Cass." Be a believer that it was many weeks before Cass lived that one down. She smiled, with tears running down her cheeks, remembering.

God, how she missed him—all those years later—but so thankful that she lived in the same house that they had so lovingly built together. He was still everywhere around her, relaxing on the stone walls that he had built, trimming wild bushes on the shoreline, and purring in and out of the driveway in his favorite vehicle, his Jeep. Cass's heart still ached when she encountered a Jeep or a Pace Arrow motor home on the highway. She was very well aware that some of her memories were warm, positive, and fulfilling during some of her lonelier moments.

After their retirement, they had traveled throughout the Orient, South America, and Europe. Cass was fascinated with London. They had dined at Le Gavroche, Bill Bentley's, and Coin de Feu, had an unforgettable seafood dinner at Prunier's on St. James Street, attended auctions at Christie's and Southeby's, shopped at Harrod's and Fortnum and Mason's, and had browsed among the books at Hatchard's and Foyles and H. W. Smith's. They found that airports were fun, too—Heathrow (London), Barajas (Madrid), Templehorf (Berlin), and even the Leonardo da Vinci, with its general and incurable inefficiency. The most unusual was Shipol in Amsterdam, where farming took place between the runways, but they would never forget Kaitak Airport on the China coast, the Kowloon side of Hong Kong. Kowloon, freely translated from the Chinese, is nine dragons, the nine hills on which that part of the city is located.

It seemed that the time spent in the Kremlin in Moscow was the one everyone back home wanted to hear about. It was a great irony that the Kremlin was populated by a regime that embraced atheism, yet within its walls was a network of old structures that recalled the passionate faith of the Russian soul. Walking across the Kremlin grounds, one can see separate churches honoring the Archangel Michael, the Twelve Apostles, the Dormition of the Virgin, and the Annunciation. Additionally there is the Church of the Deposition of the Virgin's Robe, as well as the Wall Towers dedicated to St. Peter, St. Nicholas, and the Savior. And there was the statue of Lenin to complement the mausoleum that holds his waxy, embalmed remains. But by and large, the Kremlin grounds were dominated by beautiful old churches capped with onionlike domes.

The Moscow metro system, in general, and the Komsomolskaya station, in particular, best demonstrated how aberrations could appear in Russia when one least expected them. While some American cities' subways are known for vigilantes, graffiti, and crime, Komo looked like a grand opera house transplanted underground—clean as a hound's tooth. A string of elaborate chandeliers hung from marble archways, lighting frescoes and intricate mosaics depicting scenes of Russian history—a spellbinding scene when experienced for the first time.

Rubber-capped camera lenses were seen protruding from the wall. Each person was required to put his eye against the rubber cap while a strobe flash was triggered and an electronic photograph of his retina was taken. The pattern of retinal blood vessels on the back side of the eyeball is as distinctive as a fingerprint—each one matched in an historical computer file.

But the most impressive and memorable visit was right here in Washington, D.C. The headquarters of naval intelligence occupies the entire fifth floor of the sprawling Pentagon, an enclave in the middle of the largest office building in the world, with seventeen miles of corridors and thousands of military and civilian employees. It was a gripping and proud experience to have dinner in the center yard of the Pentagon, at the Ground Zero Cafe, so named because it was once thought that the Pentagon was where the first nuclear bomb attack against the United States would take place. It was on that same trip that Cass met a publisher at the Stork Club in New York sitting at table fifty of the Cub Room, where gravitated the most important men in the world—Hollywood magnates, newspaper and book publishers, bankers, politicians, and celebrities of all kinds—the international who's who.

Other whirling pictures scampered through her

mind, some of them all too clear, others seemed to curl and blur about the edges like old letters. But what was important was that they were always together. Being on the high seas somewhere in the Windward Passage when the submarine, Thresher, went down to her death with friends aboard, the silent toast and farewell drink, tossing their highball glasses overboard from the Italian cruise-line ship, the Riviera, was totally unforgettable. Cass remembered the hours when the wives watched the harbor in Miami, waiting for a trickle of smoke from the stack of their destroyer to let them know in which order their ship would dock. It made a difference whether the husbands would be coming ashore at one, two, three, four, five, or six o'clock.

Cass's most amusing faux pas was—oh, so innocently—calling the commodore one evening to borrow shoulder boards. Rex had left his aboard ship. The commodore, a good friend, was a full commander (three stripes), and Rex, only one and a half at the time. The naivete of a fairly junior and new navy wife was the talk of the evening. The commodore had offered one shoulder board, as one and a half and one and a half make three, but did not think that our ship's captain would approve, as he carried only two and a half stripes.

Neither would her mind release the treasured memories of the days, when repairs were completed in Miami, of following the *Bernadou* along the causeway until she disappeared over the horizon. So many pictures to review, so many slide lectures for the area schools, and so many college reunions had kept Rex alive for Cass even though the illumination of love had physically gone out of her life. *Why* had God taken Rex before he had gained the strength to return to her? *Why* had God let him suffer so much? Everyone makes regrettably wrong choices sometime in his life. Why did Rex have to pay such a price for his? But all that was before Cass had become a clay pigeon. Delving into the past had, at times, rendered extremely excruciating pain, but now to the future. Cass could wait no longer to put it in writing. The desire was intense, and the motivation there.

The Clay Pigeon

1

"So you pay some bearded creep sixty an hour to tell you that you are having an anxiety attack? At which corner did he set up his little office and how long ago?"

"But, Cass, these sessions seem to make sense. I leave the appointments so much more relaxed and in control."

"In control of what, kid? Why don't you push your own computer key that says, 'Who gives a sweet rat's posterior?' and take it from there. No one can hurt you unless you let them know."

Cassandra and Susan had been through this same scenario dozens of times before; in the morning with tea, in the afternoon with something tall and cold or on the rocks, and usually with brandy following dinner, if they bothered to eat at all. They had both been through the divorce bit, but for different reasons. Sue had initiated her "freedom" and was still hurting. Cass had been rejected with no warning. They both seemed to be surviving—loners now—with the frantic search for attachments behind them.

The singles scene had left Cass with an abiding sympathy and compassion for those still playing the dating game. Would it take other pigeons as long as it took her to recognize the essence of the majority who attended singles dances? When would they realize that booze injects courage into the socially fainthearted, but that it impairs judgment, too, leaving the floor positively littered with banana skins for the unwary? She shuddered at the remembrance of the stag line, a mass of wenchers and carousers who pictured themselves as prize stallions in a paddock. Cass had been convinced that the intelligence of the whole mob could be determined by dividing the lowest IQ present by the number of the mob. She was convinced that if most of the group had any brains, they would be dangerous.

But there was deeply embedded bitterness there, too, which she thought she had overcome. Usually around four o'clock in the afternoon, any day and every day, the aching despair needed to be shared. It was one of those days that Sue again dared to offer the advice that Cass *really* needed professional help....

"This one is not a bearded creep, Cass, she is in our age bracket and has been through it all herself. It would not hurt you one iota to talk with her. Amy is a true professional, and because she *is* female, there is not that danger of falling in love with your therapist, a quicksand pit for many of us who are struggling. I have been *there,* too, but Dr. Amy Fielding has brought many back to reality. Please give her a chance?"

"I'll file that under H for Help, but putting it all in print at the moment seems to answer my need for the time being. How about settling down, Sue, and scanning my feeble attempts at putting it all on paper? Then I just might take it all to your friend Amy to see what she can glean from it."

"Holy Toledo! Cass, you said that no one would ever read this except the publisher. Mix me a really rugged drink, and find something to do while I read about your clay pigeon. And please stay off the phone. You know damn well we'll both be in trouble if we start—have another drink, get snorkered, whatever. Then I'll join you and offer my considered opinion of your efforts. And don't talk now. I'll take the recliner."

2

Cass's comments on the single life unfolded:

You know them. The jungle out there is teeming with the type—lonely, desperate for affection and understanding, searching for the truth, at least, someone to trust. Are you one of them? Haven't you discovered yet that the frantic escape to singles' bars, cruises, escort services, and lonely hearts' clubs have brought to the surface more of the same—for both the hunter and the hunted? Both genders, male and female, make up that vast gaggle of gun-carriers and their prey. *Consider!* Are *you* a clay pigeon? How many times have you been shot down?

When the workers for the city directory knock on the door to ask your status, you have to admit that you are alone, . . . another steamroller has left you completely demolished. Emerging from the chrysalis of safety to be a target for more delusions seems an insurmountable task. You have met someone whom you have trusted completely, only to find out that all that you gave of yourself was being shared with other available marks. You have been juggled enough in that market to find that you are competing with much younger pigeons, wives, ex-wives, mistresses, and jail bait.

You have tried opening the door slightly, praying that some ray of hope would present itself, then slammed it shut after another marksman had slithered through. Alcohol and tranquillizers appear to be an easier way out. *Are they?* You are saturated with psychotherapy books, self-help books, and TCP (trash can philosophy). You want to crawl back into a protective cocoon, not caring whether or not the wounds heal, don't you? Don't let it be too late for you. Just possibly, you are approaching a situation comparable to Cass's dilemma. Read it carefully. Be forewarned. Use your power of choice wisely before it is *too late*.

The next time you venture out of the nest, try to watch and listen. Just wait, watch, and listen. Listen, observe, then react, not vice versa. There are hundreds of battered souls in every walk of life. Cass's battering broke the mold, the only one, or so it seemed to her.

When he picked her off the trash heap of humankind, there was nothing in the black refrigerator except dog food, brandy, milk, and ice cubes. Cass had reached the lowest ebb of what had been an exciting and diversified life. Giving birth to an illegitimate child at the tender age of nineteen was not standard background for an embryonic schoolteacher. She was to reflect on this often, while attempting to absorb theories of educated ergots in the halls of ivy, while circulating among the VIPs of the United States Navy, while sitting among respected law makers during the sessions of the state legislature as well as the United States Congress, and while traveling throughout the world—always first class. It was a world of grace and privilege, inhabited by the elegant aristocracy of success and wealth, as well as birth. With the peasant group, propriety was despised. Here, it was everything. There were boors, fools, and drunkards among them, of course, but even when they broke the rules, the rules were valued all the same.

It seemed a ceaseless source of amazement that a life that had begun in a small town in New England was to end, by choice, in close proximity to the same area. A lovable black spaniel and a new friend had kept her alive for some months, but the hurt was too deep for her to even want to survive. No matter how hard Cass tried to understand the reasons for her situation, they got lost in the masquerade. The new friend, supposedly a mentor, who had a vast and deep and profound understanding, kept bouncing back into her life at unusual times, but all his attempts to save a life were futile. Too many small town, provincial, autocratic males (some highly intelligent, some not), who seemingly had a need to direct other people's lives, had deeply affected her life. The innate demand of such individuals plus their consuming jealousy of more materially successful females, such as the aggressive and well-endowed Cass was, in retrospect, amusing to her, although admittedly, those types had come close at times to making her life miserable. During the period of educating the offspring of others, however, those incidents were short-lived.

Cass recognized the drive for power by those chauvinistic martinets. Becoming part of the administration in a rural area school system was some individual's idea of power—how naive. But that type had never been exposed to other ways of life, other cultures, or other governments. Those who ventured out of New England always found themselves involved with people of their own kind, a security which they needed while wielding the whip over those lower in the pyramid. A wart hog had more going for it than most of those who sat on their collective and exalted asses and did nothing at all.

Too many things had happened for which Cass had no name. She had seen enough and been hurt enough to sit down and write a book, putting to use those unwritten thoughts skulking around in her head, possibly for those who were left behind to find her picture on the back of a dust jacket. That lady knew that it was too late to consider any other alternative. That gaping void in the fabric of her life was an unendurable sense of loss. While waiting to put her life in order before attempting to solve life's greatest mystery, she simply broke time into little pieces and, as with dog biscuits, all day long nibbled on half hours and their crumbs, the brittle minutes between people and activity, life and death.

Her husband, the man she depended upon (color him gone), had given her years of happiness. The divorce was a poor reward that brought nothing but misery and dissatisfaction. She still loved him and wanted him to be happy. Nothing else mattered except that. For a long time she could not sleep at all, thinking of the past and all their finest hours. At some isolated moment before dawn on one of those sleepless nights, just as one knows a fact for no logical reason, Cass knew that she would never remarry. Being well aware that she was too strong-willed for most men, she wondered vaguely whether she would ever take a lover. Somewhere in the dregs of humanity, there must be a man who didn't dribble affection like a puppy, someone who was considerate, communicative, honest, sincere, flexible, and with a high degree of sensitivity.

For months Cass felt herself quite alone and simply bore the cross as best she could—silence, the endless numbing silence, from which there was no escape, no release. She must occupy herself with something, she told herself over and over again. She must keep busy. She must fill up those empty hours or go mad. Helplessness and an overwhelming sense of failure completely veiled her thought processes.

At the beginning of that traumatic period, anger barely left room for grief, anger directed at herself for being so stupid and naive. Finally a combination of alcohol and sedatives, resulting in paroxysms of bitterness and rage, drove away her best friends. She did not want sympathy. The only one she loved was gone. She did not want to be reminded of what was left, being well aware of all that remained for her—loneliness, old age, and death. What a prospect!

For years, the marriage, for better or worse, had been recognized as a fait accompli. Dwelling in the past was a fruitless effort to understand. Certainly the stage had been set for them to quarrel over the interfering bitch. But the stage need never have been used if a number of unforeseeable circumstances had not emerged to draw them remorselessly from the wings. His kindness and concern lacked spontaneity; when examined they fell apart. He was a private person, very self-contained. Because he could withdraw for long periods to absorb himself in work, he assumed that other people did not need him any more than he needed them.

Of course, Cass could fly into a rage and act like a monster in a melodrama, but she was, she thought, a practical woman and neither so dishonest nor so proud that she could not admit the failure was not of just one alone, but theirs.

Her new mentor had introduced philosophy into that life of despair. Every night and many days were spent trying to drown in books that attempted to offer peace of mind and a will to live. While reading, her mind was absorbed in trying to discard negatives. During those hours, Cass seemed to advance into a higher level of consciousness, to begin to think positive, to count her blessings, to go another mile. Invariably, the gray light of dawn shattered all. Her only inner peace was found in the company of her mentor. His love and compassion for a floundering soul seemed to encircle Cass in a halo of hope. Those encounters did not need to consist of any more than his presence, a warm, lovable, understanding tranquillizer.

One of their conversations was a marathon of fourteen hours. Midway through that meeting, Cass knew that if she asked him what day it was, he would lecture her on the history of the calendar. But much of his conversation and advice resoundingly echoed. "Cass, you must realize that right now you are one of those who are emotionally impoverished, which is frequently more devastating that financial poverty. It is time that you become aware that unbridled emotionalism leads to disaster. You alone don't have a corner on the market of loneliness and despair in this universe. You must come face to face with yourself, come in contact with your own loneliness, your own abyss of uncertainty, your own hatred and impatience. And, Cass, never overlook *the truth,* because, properly handled, it can be an effective weapon. But at the same time, bear in mind that weapons get blunted with overuse. You'll have to use your own judgment on that decision. I still contend that when all else fails, one should try the truth. It works."

My sage friend seemed to have a hard core of practical understanding when it came to what made people tick, as he accented his advice with, "You must understand that all this does not come from experience, just an insatiable habit of reading."

Other visits amounted to a few drinks, very few for her mentor. If Cass offered a third or fourth drink, his answer would be, "No, thanks. My brain likes to know what my mouth is doing." Then he would proceed chatting about the trivia of the day or hours since they had last met, then sleep. Even while he slept, Cass's home seemed warmer, and life not nearly so threatening. Her mentor was a tired man, a hard worker, one who had been kicked exceptionally hard, but strong enough to rise above his hurts and meet life face to face. Two wives had deserted him. Keeping a home for his two sons, domestically as well as financially, without the warmth of a woman's presence was a challenge in itself. But he still found time to try to help a desperately lonely woman. That did not go unappreciated. Cass knew that taking her life was poor compensation for his efforts. She also knew that it would also be a disappointment in the judgment of God. She was ashamed of her weakness but determined to depart. Hell was right here on earth.

Cass's only hope was the companionship of her mentor on a permanent basis—a crutch of constancy. But that was an impossibility. His life had been interrupted by their chance meeting, and his life would go on. The problems of Cass were a burden to him, she knew. Trying to change the waste materials of humankind by attempting to give a new sense of hope and direction and striving to help her return from living death was extremely taxing. She tried to agree that everyone is a special creation of God. She sensed what her new friend counted on, that every individual had a pilot light burning inside them that never goes out. That as long as there is a breath of life remaining, there is hope. He was a man who had done time on human trash heaps and walked away from his own grave. He admittedly had stumbled at times but innately knew that only he had the ultimate decision of how his life would be lived. It seemed that he had chosen to live by one of the philosophies of Marcus Aurelius, "Be like the promontory against which the waves constantly break, but it stands firm and tames the waters around it."

After five months of his company, Cass realized that she was becoming more and more dependent upon her mentor and confidant for her happiness. She was deeply aware that her thoughts seemed to coincide with a definition by Norman Vincent Peale, "Happiness is an antidote...something that will help us deal with our problems so that we will not resign from the human race—and the ultimate form of resignation is suicide."

Until that move was made, the situation had to change... Why? His face, his voice, his charismatic manner intruded into whatever she was doing or thinking and wiping out all concentration. Whenever he left her to go about his own affairs, she had a premonition hovering, making an abortive attempt to filter through her drugged mental wanderings, a forewarning that the relationship would hurt her more than the present burden she was carrying. Cass recognized the positive move to solve the problem—*replace!* But she did not want to leave the mental house clean of one demon, only to have another one move in when she left that house empty.

It was time that a bit of self-analysis was in order, now that there was no one to hurt by the disclosure of her past mistake—an illegitimate child released for adoption. A heart-wrenching decision. What had led her to that point?

3

Cass had been the third child of four, always living under the shadow of her siblings. An older brother, first-born, eventually proved to be her only trusted friend in the family. The second birth was a sister, one who had been jealous and destructive of others' rights and opinions all her life, precocious and much more vindictive as an adult, who despised her own father and obviously her younger sister. It was three years later that Cass, the winsome one, appeared on the scene, during the dark depression years of the 1920s. Due to the financial situation, she was initiated into always receiving the crumbs, the cast-off toys, bicycles, clothing, and it seemed to her, affection. Possibly that drove her to a future of searching for a warm and dependable relationship with someone to whom she would not have to play second fiddle. Possessiveness? Very likely.

As a child, Cass spent her time with animals and books. The stray cats that she brought home always "ran away," later to be found at the local horse farm. The solace of books and solitude of the fields and woods were her escapes in her early teens. The high school days were filled with a scholastic grind, leaving no time for dating, even if it had not been a taboo in the family household at the time. Cass was only fifteen years of age upon graduating from the local academy, very naive, introspective, and completely satisfied with her own choices. Twice during her senior year at the academy, she had had confrontations with the opposite sex. Those experiences had left her terrified of boys and their cravings and disgust with the male species in general.

College and campus life was a whole new world. It was there that Cass met the boy with whom, in retrospect, she should have spent the rest of her life. He was a true friend of comparable background and interests with whom she spent the better part of four unforgettable years. World War Two was raging, bringing forth many glamorous uniforms. When a handsome and fun-loving naval officer offered his attentions, dating a college boy seemed exceptionally mundane. Marriage and travel were proposed. It was then that Cass began the pattern of using her power of choices unwisely, the first of many wrong choices.

At that tender age, she found herself married to a man about whom she knew and understood little. Following a brief but glamorous honeymoon, there was a period of nearly a year when the U. S. Navy chose to send her husband to the Pacific War theater. Again alone and lonely, the days were passed with an attempt at putting to use her training as a teacher. The daylight hours were not too difficult to handle. It was the many nights, which seemed to close in. On one of those haunting dusk to dawn eons, Cass found herself back in the arms of her college friend, her first love. That insatiable need for affection led into another wrong choice, a deeply emotionally charged episode—adultery. By that time, her college friend was in uniform—seemingly a weakness with Cass. That wrong use of her power of choice resulted in the conception of a child.

For weeks Cass carried that burden of guilt—again *alone*. Her love of children and an intrinsic desire for a warm, lasting relationship had to be submerged. That God-given life within her womb had to be destroyed. Abortion? Murder in her opinion at such an early age. Again the manifestation of not using her power of choice wisely.

Abortion clinics had not yet come into existence. No doctor or other medical person would even listen to her plea. The secret search for a naturopath was a terrifying one, but her efforts uncovered what was the answer to her dilemma. Abortion was *not* the answer. She would have the baby as soon as she found a home that would care for her during her pregnancy. She had solved the problem, but the payment was to sign a release form agreeing to give up her baby permanently. Cass could see no other way out. Her husband was overseas at the time of conception and would not return for many months, or so she hoped. That was the chance she had to take, the only solution.

The pregnancy followed its normal course, and with an excruciatingly painful birth, she delivered a beautiful baby boy. But he was no longer hers. She saw him fleetingly, and was so very, very thankful that she had not snuffed out his life. Knowing that she would never, never forget him, and in her mind, she gave him the name of Archer. That little soul, God's creation, most probably would have been the one who could have kept Cass on course, to help her fulfill her reason for being, her reason for not being a disappointment to all who picked her up when she stumbled.

Thoughts of the past kept a persistent battering against her attempt to accept the higher truth that she instinctively knew could save her. It became obvious that the willingness to contact the Higher Power must include the strength to do it, that that Power would come only when she would admit to her own helplessness. She must see this simply as a fact, with neither shame nor despair. She was beginning to believe what the New Testament meant by losing life in order to find it. Willingness did not mean strength; it meant only a definite decision to change the direction of her life. She was convinced that one need not know everything in order to start favoring oneself. She did not need to understand the secret process by which air refreshed the body. She needed only to breathe. Furthermore, a concerted effort was made to accept one of those, which seemed to her, contradictions of life: "If you do not strain your mind, it will contact the Higher Power that works through you and for you."

Unfortunately those insights did not register too deeply. Unconsciously, Cass sought revenge toward the man who had deserted her to marry her sister. The search for a whole new life was approached through the wrong channels. Add another misuse of her power of choice—a frantic social life among total strangers. Women and their constant prattle had always been the depth of boredom to Cass. The male world seemed much more interesting. Actually, for many years, she had not really listened to anyone. That did not become a reality to her until her mentor suggested that she stop bemoaning her plight and start *listening* to all conversations. If one listened carefully, the verbalizing, for the most part, consisted of dialogues of the deaf.

Indeed, very few exchanges of opinion proved to be a real desire to understand the other person. Having worked with children in a guidance capacity, she recalled her advice to others: "No one can find the peace and serenity of a meaningful life without feeling understood by at least one person. When misunderstood, one totally loses his self-esteem and faith in life, even in God."

It was the ideal situation to open up to a confidant, hopefully a trustworthy one, perhaps one who would help her find Archer.

4

Possibly, had that philosophy been dredged out of her mental depths earlier, Cass would not have ended in "the jungle." The beginning of that initiation into the dog-eat-dog world was bolstered by alcohol and pills. Being basically shy, but appearing aggressive (a camouflage for her inhibitions), Cass could not face her appearances at the local singles dances twice a week without the protective umbrella of tranquilizers and brandy. She neither liked to dance nor knew how, but with her mentality blocked, she added insult to injury—*she did not care!*

The very first dance with a gentleman to whom she was slightly attracted was a shocker. Before the end of the first set, she was deeply hurt by what became a standard question from others, "Do you fool around?" The first time, Cass shrugged it off as either having been the alcohol or the lack of finesse of the individual concerned. Later that night, she laughed at that remark. She knew that she was not a tramp and that she did not present herself in such a manner.

The rules of that particular club was that one must not refuse an invitation to dance the first time invited. So much for meeting some real losers walking around in a testosterone fog. Her first reaction had been to leave the premises and never return, thinking that when you drain a swamp, you are bound to find a lot of slimy creatures. But within the week, prairie fever (which she called loneliness) set in. Her "don't give a damn" pills encouraged a phone call, and it happened! Never having been promiscuous, Cass thought that the sexual encounter would develop into a lasting relationship. How naive. She did not yet understand about clay pigeons.

The next time she met the male involved, he neither asked her to dance nor spoke to her. Shattering. So it was a matter of doubling up on the booze and tranquillizers, seeking to be brazen by ignoring the whole episode. Actually, Cass knew that that type of repression would eventually fester and explode in some manner. But outwardly, a shrug and a seemingly couldn't-care-less attitude helped her to keep slithering through her newly discovered social life. Tragic.

Other invitations were graciously refused. Some dinners with close friends and many phone calls from others not so well known ensued, but no intimate confrontations. Cass was still mentally hurting from the first one. Some men acquaintances were invited to her home, and some visited without explicit invitations, but she was able to stay outside any personal relationship, convinced that they all had a terminal Don Juan complex.

Finally, the inevitable. Cass could remember neither when nor how many pills had been popped or drinks tossed. The danger of driving under those conditions was extreme, but who cared, either for herself or for others. Those thoughts were never allowed to surface. That was a period when blackouts were almost daily occurrences. No one else seemed to be aware of the situation, and Cass *didn't care*. It was too late. She had been shot down so brutally, and her longing for Archer was constant. If only someone had reminded her that those who do not remember the past are condemned to repeat it.

One episode in particular should have jolted the most callous of individuals into reality. That mentally indelible evening, a Sunday, Cass attended church to pray for her son. Difficulty in parking the car on the street by simply parking parallel to the curb was a stab of warning. But it went unheeded. All types of breath-o-laters and mints were always available to partially cover the alcoholic fumes. The sermon was accepted by a fuzzy mind. Cass always sat in the very back corner of the church with the hope of departing without having to speak to the minister. It happened very seldom. She was convinced that the pastor had a private tunnel through which he raced to the door to greet his parishioners individually. Those courtesies resulted in the exhibition of a carefully paced exit toward her car to burn rubber for singles. Needless to say, the pastor would visit her home to try to save a soul, but those visits were a waste of time, his and Cass's. Does there exist a license to kill? Everyone at the club was friendly, and excitement high—her new acquaintances so glad to see her, like conscientious bees buzzing from flower to flower. Attention at last... the finest kind. Cass had arrived! Now the party begins.

She danced very seldom and always with the closed group at her table. One day a stranger appeared. Later, Cass found that he had been there many times before, but had gone unnoticed. Weeks later, the question often arose whether that marksman had bided his time until Cass was really floundering. A handsome, charismatic, and courteous Adonis who exuded animalistic sexual magnetism threw Cass's vows completely off center. His approach was unique, "An heiress, I understand, and I have seen you somewhere, possibly on the U.S.S. *Rotterdam?*"

That was the mother of all shockers. Not many months before, Cass had returned from a forty-two day cruise to the North Cape on its sister ship, The T.S. *Hamburg*. Her alcohol-saturated brain gave him a high rating of credibility—a mistaken opinion which persisted for many months, unfortunately.

Being asked to dance a second time by someone who

was an exceptionally good dancer was the utmost flattery. She still did not let herself accept that hers was a scene of not at all graceful stumbling.

Then the question, "Are we going to incorporate?" The same approach, but so astutely presented. To the end of time, there would be just a vague recollection of Cass's reaction. But react she did—another blackout. Fortunately for her, he was an honest man.

It was a miracle that the Thunderbird found its way home. The radio beam lifted the massive, double garage door, and in sidled the Bird, but this time, a foreign car purred softly in beside it. Later, much later, she was informed that her beloved spaniel greeted them both joyously. Drinks were mixed, and the dialogue on Cass's part appeared to be rational;. Fortunately for her, the gentleman did not choose to take advantage of a not at all reticent and thoroughly inebriated lady.

The dawning of another day found Cass stumbling toward her morning-after ice water. It was embarrassing, shocking, and terrifying to find a complete stranger in a living room chair. Who was he? From whence did he come? How long had he been there? How did he get into the house? Cass muttered a silent vow never to take another drink. Scurrying back to the bedroom for proper attire, she could not keep her imagination from running rampant over what she could remember of the night's activities. But face the foreign appearing, olive-skinned stranger she must. He certainly was fully accepted by her spaniel, who was sleeping peacefully at the stranger's feet.

Attempting to be casual, certainly not caring to admit her dilemma, Cass offered coffee and very light conversation, hoping to inadvertently shed some light on the previous evening—at least to discover his name.

5

The stranger filled her in with no holds barred. He expounded on what occurred, stressing with heavy ridicule, Cass's conduct while drinking. Without waiting to be asked his opinion, he donned his black robe and sat on the judge's bench. Proceeding to what could have taken place, he instilled in her a petrifying fear. Cass could have been left a bloody corpse, and her home stripped, as well as her fingers of hundreds of dollars worth of diamonds. When his diatribe came to an end, she felt like a delinquent child who had been severely reprimanded.

"Instant coffee?"

"Sure, if that's all you have."

"I don't have a coffee maker because I don't drink the stuff."

"You don't need a coffee maker for what you consume."

Dead silence. The only way to escape was to put the spaniel out on his run. Still silence. Gawd what crass brass, but spoken with a brilliant, tooth-flashing smile. What does one say to a total stranger? Cass did manage one sip of ice water, then placed his coffee on a nearby end table.

"Black?"

"Right."

More silence, but that was due to be shattered promptly. Scared and trembling almost uncontrollably, but undeniably curious, Cass perched on the edge of a companion chair with her rattling cup and saucer.

"Tea? That's a switch, why not a drink?"

"I don't drink in the morning."

Sarcastic as hell for an invader of her home, or was he? Perhaps she had invited him here. But let's get rid of him, then crawl way back into the foot of the bed. That didn't happen.

He exploded from his chair, pointed a giant, sausage-sized finger within inches of her nose, raging.

"Lady, I have been watching you for weeks. You are a menace to mankind. You have no right to be behind the wheel of a car. If you care nothing for your own life, what about others? How would you feel if you killed someone, possibly a whole family, or adults leaving some children with no parents?" He had no idea how that question painfully knifed directly through her heart. She had left Archer with no parents and was still hurting deeply. All this attempt at discipline was in anything but a conversational tone of voice. It sounded to Cass like shattering machine-gun fire.

"And furthermore, I will repeat, you could have been left here battered to a pulp, including the dog, with the house totally trashed, and no one would have ever known *why* or *who*! You have no idea who I am, but it's lucky for you that I am who I am."

"Who are you?" She was completely intimidated, but damned if she would cry.

"I have told you a number of times, but apparently, it doesn't get through that cloud you drift around in. Can't you remember?"

Spilling a goodly portion of her tea, Cass nodded yes.

"When did you eat last? There's nothing in the refrigerator except dog food and ice cubes."

"Right."

"Will you eat with me if I bring in something? I saw a store nearby and would like to concoct an omelet." Cass turned away and gagged, but nodded affirmatively. This just might be her chance to get out of this situation.

"And furthermore, don't even consider disappearing, because I have the keys to your vehicle, and I doubt whether you are in any condition to locate a second set. Ten to one you don't even know where your purse is. Don't waste your time hunting for it, as I have put it away and will give it to you when I return. Could you manage a cold shower while I am gone? You're a mess, like something the cat would be ashamed to drag in. Get the dog in, too." As soon as the spaniel was inside, he left.

Makeup smeared and hair tangled, who the hell cared, she'd probably never see him again anyway, as well as her purse. She opened the kitchen curtains to watch him leave. It seemed odd that he knew that he could walk to the market. But he did, wearing a black leather jacket. "Oh, please God, not a motorcyclist!" When he disappeared from sight, past her driveway, Cass furtively sneaked a peek in the garage. What unmitigated nerve! There was his sports car. At least he wasn't a biker. Either he had expensive taste or he knew good cars. But how did he get the automatic door down? How did he find the switch? Maybe she did it. Total blank. Out-of-state license plate, "Maybe he lives far away; hope so, or do I?"

Cass had just time enough to shower, remove all makeup and brush her hair—still a morning after disaster. *Blue,* put on something blue. It might help.

Back he came, charging through the door and directly to the kitchen, taking over completely, making himself totally at home. That was a plus. Cooking was of no interest to Cass whatsoever. In fact, she smiled as she remembered being told that the only thing domestic about her was that she was born in this country.

"Please make only enough for yourself. All I can handle is hot tea and maybe a slice of dry toast right now."

"What would you have had if I weren't here? Another drink probably. There wasn't even any bread in the house."

"Oh?"

His actions were fascinating. He did look like an Adonis. Not very tall, about five feet ten, expensive Bally shoes, navy blue cashmere V-necked sweater, pale blue open-necked shirt, gray flannels, and *no* white socks, navy blue. Thank God, no white socks. And no rings—love of God, where were her rings? The watch was still on her wrist, but no rings! They could be anywhere. Did she dare ask?

"You threw your rings in the ashtray last night"—mental telepathy or unnoticed observance? "They are on your dresser. You really don't give a damn, do you. You have no business wearing jewelry like that in the places you frequent."

The omelet was beautifully served even with a sprig of parsley. Cass tried to eat, but after two bites, a dash to barf.

"I do apologize, you have gone to so much trouble. But I don't usually eat much until later."

"Sure, like after how many drinks? I won't be here later."

"Why not? You certainly haven't come to a screeching halt to enumerating my faults and frailties." Cass felt guilty about reacting with sarcasm to all his efforts. "Why are you here if I am such a threatening, disintegrating mess, such a disgusting example of humanity?"

"To help you if at all possible. I think you need a friend. You are a *mark,* bombing about in a new Thunderbird, wearing hundreds of dollars worth of jewelry, and living alone in a home like this. You need to listen."

He was talking about clay pigeons, but Cass didn't recognize the analogy at the time. This was the beginning of a whole new experience, in retrospect, a whole new life!

But he also listened. His warmth and understanding of Cass's personal problems were profoundly sincere, with deep empathy for her past abusive treatment and present mental torment. This was the beginning of many weeks of enjoyment interwoven with constant therapy, advice, and philosophy. This was a whole new interesting world, a replacement for her deep sense of loss—*until*....

She was replaced, shot into fragments again. Strangely enough, it was an even deeper sense of loss, but the law of cause and effect operated true to form. Cass looked within. The association with her new friend had to cease. It hurt too much, and the loneliness had returned. She purposely delved into his liaisons with other women, and there were many. None of her business? Correct. She knew that. But she also knew that she was forcing herself to break a damaging relationship. She had begged her mentor to literally tell her to get off his case. This he refused to do, probably knowing that she would be found near death somewhere, but too late. The clay pigeon would be totally shattered and scattered by the ill winds of more wrong choices.

He had saved her life once by interrupting a suicide attempt, resulting in his not daring to be as brutal as she begged him to be. She would never erase the picture in her mind of him stroking his beard, tilting his head while uplifting his palms, and smiling in his oblique way. His guidance and affection would always be with her. In that aspect, he would never leave her.

Religion did not seem to be the answer. Meditation did help her to recall past involvements with men. At the time, each one had seemed to be her answer to total fulfillment. But each time, they had been eventually forgotten and pushed into the past by Cass's changeable inconstancy and capriciousness of the true Gemini. Would she ever find someone with whom she could share greater sincere rapport and compatibility and, more important, would understand her longing to know something of Archer's present life?

Following her divorce, Cass had met many men during her travels throughout the world, all disappointments. One air force colonel had seemed to be the answer, but after five months, he had been sent overseas for an extended tour of duty. Just as well. The drinks he mixed would dissolve anyone's intestines, and booze had taken quite a toll on his veracity. She could still smile, thinking that when she first met him, his eyes were so blue that he probably drank Tidy Bowl, then washed his eyes out with Mercurochrome the next morning. Really, his liver would more likely burn longer and brighter than the Olympic Flame. She also recalled that he had to shave using both hands. That affair quietly waned.

A liquor distillery official appeared on the scene, one who was adept at courting, wining, and dining, the whole dating scene. But an institutionalized wife hovered on the horizon. And in conjunction with that, Cass had too much compassion for others to intentionally hurt anyone. That relationship was cut cleanly by suggesting to him that his problem was midlife crisis, resulting in a brutally damaged ego. But it worked. She was free to play the field again.

6

Ready to freshen her drink, Sue rattled her ice cubes and headed for the bar.

"My God, Cass, in all our mind meanderings, you have never mentioned this paragon of masculinity. And a son named Archer, come on, cut the comedy, or is this fictional just to keep the reader interested?"

"Read on, kid, there's more, much more. Your Dr. Amy Fielding will have a field day with this stuff. Although she may have faced worse."

"Cass, when I finish this, can we talk? This gives me the courage to admit to some antics of my own that I have never been able to share, even with Amy."

"Sure, but as I said, read on, and don't get so bombed that you will forget what you want to share. I'll listen and promise not to be judgmental."

Sue's drink remained on the end table ignored and untouched after the first sip. Watching Sue squirm, swipe at an intermittent tear, and occasionally gasp with definitely recognizable expletives, punctuated with deep whimpering sighs, Cass mixed another drink, vowing that she must quit these velvet hammers. Eggnog and brandy were proving to be too damned fattening, but she also had to be careful not to get the ulcers romping. She was fast approaching the don't-give-a-damn stage.

"Well are you reading the mess twice? I didn't ask you to edit it, I just want an opinion," she muttered.

Sue practically burst from the lounger.

"Phew, Cass, how in the hell have you survived all this? Two marriages and two heavy, heavy affairs, to say nothing of the interim episodes from which you have been able to escape. All this, so far, is more than most poor souls would experience in two lifetimes. Having really 'been there,' you could take over Dr. Amy's office anytime, considering that you seem to have learned something from your passages in and out of love. Really, what general advice would you offer to people who are just starting out in this jungle, alone, especially regarding how to handle men?"

"Sue, my friend, you have met a few of the types, and for sure, both of us will meet others. I can only suggest that from the beginning of a friendship, *be yourself* and *be honest* without divulging everything about yourself and your past. Men do love mystery, some more, some less. Try always to leave something to the imagination. If the particular guy involved hasn't the ability or sense of fun to fantasize, then he's missing a big part of life. But always remember, *that's his problem.*"

"It's uncanny that now you seem to be able to spot the sincerely lonely and nice guys and separate them from the lotharios who are looking for new clay pigeons. What's your secret?"

"You know as well as I, Sue, that there are definite degrees of both. Let's kick around a few. It has been my experience that the singles' standards are basically trashy—not all, just the majority. They have acquired their freedom from the drudgery of a wife, kids, dogs, lawn mowers, and schedules. They are ready to spout the statistics on the percentage of available men to single women. They love that, and many are certain that they are the answer to all lonely women's prayers. Gawd, how disgusting. Most of them would fall off their perch if not nailed to it.

"Sure, they know the lonely ones, and they prey upon them by listening, sympathizing, advising, and offering affection. The majority are also looking for a nest, or possibly just a place to hang out, especially if the pigeon is ready, willing, and able to cook. If a roll in the hay is available, so much the better. Some of us are stronger than others, Sue, and I'm not sure what your problems are. To date, our conversations have been random ramblings, and I fail to see that your vital signs have ever dwindled."

"But after the kind of treatment that you've survived, how can you tell me that to keep a relationship healthy, I must never complain, criticize, or condemn. Bullshit! It would seem easier to get a dog. At least they know nothing about lies and deceits and only fight to protect what they love. How can you still be sensitive and accepting and *not* be critical? That sounds like playing God."

Cass did not react immediately.

"Yup, I have to admit, if you want loyal, get a cocker spaniel." After some thought, she did suggest that Sue elaborate on at least one of her experiences, then promised to attempt some suggestions through which Sue could sift.

"It just might be Cass, that I can open up to you more than to the shrink. Dr. Amy's a great gal, but I doubt whether she has struggled with anything comparable to your hurts. She still seems to think that making a success of your single life is the best revenge—I'm still floundering. Her comments are repeatedly that there is nothing more tedious than the obvious. How can we spot the obvious when we're totally hooked?

"Okay, Cass, for a change of pace, kick this one around." Sue proceeded to expose the ugly truth of her last involvement. "I was sickly hooked. At the time, I was spinning in a whirlpool, brain detonated, unable to concentrate on anything except his beauty and skill and what he was doing to me. I was one throbbing nerve end, and he knew just which switches to flick and buttons to press. Many nights I lay pondering on what was happening to me. I was changing, no doubt about it. I won't say that I was naive prior to this affair, but I was inclined to accept people at their face value, believing what they told me.

"I suppose I had lived a more or less sheltered existence. Womanizing and the new sexual freedom were things I read about or saw on television. But following those weeks I became intimately acquainted with what I call the underbelly of life. People *did* lie. They were not what they seemed. And they were capable of acting irrationally, driven by passions that they could not control. That experience added evidence of how often the heart and glands overruled the mind and good sense. By now I should be wiser, more cynical, and street smart, but dammit, I'm not.

"And I really have hurt more over this one than any that I have become involved with before, Cass, and there have been a few. But he was a physically gorgeous man and an athlete on a water bed. He had absorbed somewhere that, for starters, the best way to seduce a woman was to make her laugh, and he had a helluva sense of humor. He seemed intelligent, was charming and mercurial enough to be appealing. He owned a boat and could cook. What more could I have wanted? But, lady, was I ever wrong. He turned out to be a real lightweight, a true tripper. He wouldn't have known a Ming vase from a Tupperware container. If he had any capacity for emotional commitment to anything or anyone, he never revealed it to the female population. I certainly don't prefer solemn men, but I do like a soupçon of seriousness now and then.

"He seemed to float through life, bobbing on the current. Everything was a joke, and laughter was the medicine that cured all. But he was good company and gave me a lift at the time. I can't deny that. The problem was that when we were naked and floundering around in the water bed, he was an entertainer. I didn't want to think of how many women he had been with to learn all the tricks that he knew. He certainly educated me. He was such an expert but always separated, not really involved, like an actor who had played the scene too many times. Still I could not escape. Why didn't someone or something shoot me down in time? He was all over me with his wicked tongue and absolutely no inhibitions.

"I responded in the same manner, of course. Don't you try to adopt the customs of the natives when in a foreign country? Each time I was reasonably certain that I was a candidate for intensive care, but he was skilled enough to hold me in a warm, relaxing hug, keeping me purring. He didn't miss a trick. Too many had cared for him too much, when he cared for no one, not even himself, actually, or he would have been his own man and not a gigolo, an icy sociopath totally lacking in conscience.

"But hey, Cass, I'm leaving your problems. Let me get back to your manuscript, and we'll kick around that Marquis Mouse of mine later. I should have tied a knot in his glands, what is left of them, or kept his scrotum and tacked it to the wall."

7

Sue settled in with Cass's manuscript.

A professional baseball player held her interest for a short period, but alcohol had taken priority in his life, too. He was another member of that well-known genus, a compulsive philanderer who imagined that his goal in life was to brighten with his horizontal favors every woman he met. She didn't need that. Again, cut!

Then the Arab, the biggest mistake of all. If she could have accepted his attention as love and compassion for a suffering human being, the friendship might have been a lasting one. Unfortunately, emotions took over, which were leading nowhere. But she did marvel that he found her interesting enough to spend a piece of his busy life with her—the basic working tool of a top-level con artist. Again, her power of choice used wrongly. She should have alienated him before she became totally hooked. She should have checked it off as a one-act tragedy.

Possibly, travel would help Cass get it together. She did mix easily with people from all walks of life. Her time spent in Russia and behind the Iron Curtain in Berlin had left her with a gently nagging longing to return, to become better acquainted with the philosophy of those people.

Cass knew that it was only the knowledgeable and clever ones whose folly can make them wise or produce good results, the sampling of all kinds of work and cultures may be part of everybody's education if they so choose. One learns an enormous amount that way, about skills and organizations, about all kinds of people and their ways of thinking. There were facets about her travels that she liked and many that she didn't like at all, things that she detested and things which she passionately favored. There were things which she had seen in her travels that seemed to make good sense and things that filled her with disgust. She had come to believe that people are both the victims and the beneficiaries of their breeding. It nips them in the bud, but it also may bring them to blossom. How, she often wondered, can one minimize the nippings, avoid the cankers, and make the individual bloom more beautifully? That was the big question.

Some months later, another morning dawned with the brash realization that she was still hooked—the brutal truth. Icicles of reality stabbed at Cass's heart, already scarred with the many stitch marks of past wounds. She had acquired a habit, a dangerous one. Unconsciously, the Arab had become the axis upon which she spun, a very necessary part of her life. She was hooked to the degree of not being the same person that she had been before meeting him. Nothing and no one held even a spark of interest. In fact, friends of many years' standing were avoided. Long vigils by the telephone were eroding, yes, dissipating her life.

Her future without him seemed bleak, and weeks were passing by, not slowly and contentedly, but like being smothered under a landslide. The realization that something must be done hammered her dangerously toward the brink. That long ribbon of highway toward an inevitable chasm of pain must have a crossroad somewhere. Knowing that all that heavy construction must be battled alone, Cass forced herself to take a long, hard look at the alternatives. The present route was only leading to disaster, she being the single casualty.

It must be done—an achingly painful exploration of the affair, a dissecting and stripping of the actions and character of the man involved. She must face the facts of exactly what he had to offer her—a future of sharing him with other women (a sick addiction), a life heavily seasoned with agony or *flight*. The torture, suffering, and torment must come to a halt somehow. Flight to emotional freedom was a misty goal, but it seemed at the time the only chance for survival.

Cass reflected on the fact that she had been told by her paramour that he was emotionally and morally involved with another. She admired his "complete honesty," so she stumbled along under the false illusion of hope that his interest in his other enterprise would wane. The reality was an unending trail of other women. Why could she not accept the opinions of those who had met him—a psychotic sociopath, a Don Juan...?

Thus Cass continued to invite mental abuse. Even that at times seemed easier to cope with than sliding back into the past, to dwelling on the loss of her son, the very foundation of her life. Possibly a professional counselor could have brought forth a solution to her dilemma. Could the agony of trying to forget her husband and trying to bury thirty-two years of her life be a solvable problem? Could the Arab be an anaesthetic, a tranquillizer, a balm for the real wound that someday might heal?

Why didn't she take his advice and accept half a loaf, which was better than none? Foggily, she did have a momentary thought that that depended upon the ingredients of the loaf. Why couldn't she accept the fact that she was "wasting her time" as he had told her repetitively? Why did she listen to his constant ramblings concerning his conquests of other women, including the minute details of their association as well as their financial status? Why didn't she search for other companions, as he advised? Why did she repeatedly interfere with his private life? There seemed to be no answer—an abortive search.

Why? Why? Why? Physical torture would have been less damaging. Why did she inflict such mental anguish upon herself, something akin to self-destruction?

Rather than daring to admit that she needed help, Cass muddled along the same course, interfering with other people's lives, resorting to depths of evasiveness and cunning, scheming rather than thinking, floundering in tides of negativity and self-pity.

Knowing that she was not strong enough to bring the relationship to an end (then she would really be alone), she begged the Arab to do it, to cancel her out of his life. It would have been so much easier, but he refused to do so, directly that is. Perhaps he feared the old truth that hell hath no fury like a woman scorned, even though it was by request. Perhaps he feared the consequences of her highly unpredictable antics. Or perhaps he felt that his actions would speak more loudly than words.

During holidays, he began to be "out of town." Birthdays and anniversaries were spent with his ex-wife. Elaborations concerning the number of women that he had had and expected to have surfaced more frequently. He bragged about his eighteen-, nineteen-, and twenty-year-old coeds who could give him another family. Many attempts were made to become associated with Cass's female friends or with anyone at all appealing to whom she had introduced him, including her neighbors. These were not easy torments to handle while struggling to survive the fact that Archer, the son to whom she had given birth, was being raised by someone else, total strangers.

When one is so far down that there is no place to go but up, hopefully the spark to survive could be kindled. Cass made feeble grasps at an attempt to escape her demeaning situation. She knew that trying to surmount obstacles had been in daily practice since the beginning of time; some creative force taught the bird to balance and fly, a crab or lobster to replace a lost limb. Why could not her rational mind work with this same force? Had not the Arab explicitly told her that he did not love her, that he did have a "love and compassion" for her? Another line with a great big hook on it, placed firmly and deeply within Cass's being. Shot down again.

One day the message penetrated—tranquillizers were mind-altering drugs. Small wonder that she could neither think logically nor rely on her powers of intuition. Both had been blocked by her tiny, round white crutches fortified with alcohol.

It took many attempts and failures before the medication could be cut down. Nightmare-riddled sleep; when sleep did overtake her tattered, bloody, pulplike nerves, Cass was left constantly exhausted and disorganized. However, the ability to think rationally did surface periodically. She would recall her mother saying, "Life is what you make it." Cass would often think of a tiny grain of mustard seed enclosed in a plastic bubble dancing on a gold chain about her mother's wrist. That memory led her to ponder that master's precept, "If ye have faith as a grain of mustard seed, ye shall say unto this mountain, 'Remove hence to yonder place'; and it shall remove; and nothing shall be impossible to you." Cass did not want to remove mountains, just survive, without sorrow and loneliness compounded by a constant inner dull ache.

The psychotherapy and the myriad of self-help books advised the expelling of all negative thoughts from the mind, like shaking stones from your sandals. In the process of trying to meditate, it made sense, but in reality, the feat was much more difficult. When the final blow descended, it was impossible for anything to penetrate.

Her mentor, the Arab, upon whom she had become completely dependent, had been sincere in his truthfulness. The evidence surfaced. He really was being inti-

8

"I've read it all, Cass, and there's some really brutal hurt here. But I must say that some of your ideas sound like free, aged, horse manure. Now can I tell you about the bastard who finally did me in, physically, emotionally, and pretty damned near financially? Kid, if we don't talk this out together and get Amy's help, we are in trouble, top-notch candidates for the Primal Scream Institute. We can't sit in the lotus position for the rest of our lives, hoping that someone will untie the knot and say, 'Hey, kid, this is the way it really is!' I'm still fairly sober, I think, but despondent as hell. May I share with you right now some of what's hurting me? He's a real son of a bitch, and I should have known, but it might help to talk about it. By then the kitchen looked as though someone had detonated a hand grenade.

"Let it roll, Sue. Tell me about your stand-up nervous breakdown. As strong as you are, he must have been a real gear jammer." Cass had once seen a documentary film on open heart surgery that showed the palpitating heart muscle. That was what her head felt like at the moment, but she didn't want to derail Sue's train of thought.

"Okay, Cass, here it is, low and slow like the pilot's say. He turned my world upside down and inside out. And dammit, Cass, you and I both know that when you are a wealthy woman, you meet all sorts of characters—the wily, the money grubbers, the snobs, the hunters, and the downright crooks. I didn't want to live my life being suspicious of everyone. No, I counted people from one hundred down, not up. Instead of anticipating the worst, waiting for people to prove that they were worthy of my friendship, I did it the other way around. I expected them to be worthy and only gave them demerits when they disappointed me.

"That left me open to a lot of emotional injuries, just as it did you. But I know now how foolhardy it is to give anyone my trust until they have earned it. Amy has already told me that I should have left—no apologies, no excuses, nothing—just quietly closed the door on the involvement and left. If only I had done that. If only I had realized then that when a forbidden love creeps into your heart, the only thing to do is get rid of it, and the first step in that process is to remove yourself far from it."

"Okay, right, I have been there, too, but neither one of us had the guts to leave. We were both leaning on someone for emotional support plus having a deep desire to be needed, searching for complete and total trust and integrity. Just be thankful that we did manage to exist with a broken heart. We have to live with pain, of course, because it never seems to leave, does it. Mine is a mixture of loneliness and regret. I didn't mean to rattle on, Sue, and I promise not to interrupt again. Tell me about your paragon of sexuality."

"He is a proven manipulator and exploiter, Cass, with callouses on his hands from social climbing. When I met him, it was in the spring when I had just returned from that winter in Jamaica and anxious to show off my deep golden tan ahead of everyone else. Singles. There wouldn't be anyone there for tan competition. And there he sat, all alone and seemingly reeking of class and substance. What had to have grabbed my attention was the Harris tweed jacket with leather elbow patches. It definitely made an impression among that collection of salivating, geriatric ass-pinchers dressed in sloppy flannel shirts and enough denim to launch a cattle drive. He flashed that grand piano of his that he called a smile.

"'Hi. What brought a classy lady like you into this pit?'

"'Curiosity, perhaps, what's your reason?'

"'Cabin fever, I guess, but that can't be your problem, sporting a tan like that.'

"'Right. I should have stayed on the islands, drinking beer and eating oysters.'

"Jack was a cool customer, Cass. When he offered to buy me a drink, I thanked him, 'No thanks, I buy my own.'

"'That's a switch.'

"'Oh, then you are aware of the harpooners in a place like this!'

"A smile with an invitation to dance, a real smoothie, not the standard stomping that a stevedore would admire, but slow and easy. And no suggestion of being on the make. While sitting between dances, he seemed to have it all together, conversation-wise anyway, a reasonably rational gent with no evidence of wanting to be part of the group grope. I was impressed, Cass! Was he really an eligible, unattached bachelor? They are as rare as unicorns, as you well know. I guess I have to admit that I opened the door to all this torture, because before I wandered around doing the table-hopping thing, I did manage to jot my phone number on his raffle ticket. Mistake. He disappeared sometime during my excursion around the hall. So I thought, *What the hell, that's that.*"

"But sure enough, the phone rang the next day.

"'Thanks for making my evening. I really needed a morale booster.'

"'Aren't you going again tonight?'

"'Sure, if you'll be there.'

"Obviously, I followed up on that one. That night, the wing-tip shoes did it. Why in the hell am I so easily impressed? But again, he was not at all pushy.

"'So you like oysters? I'll make an oyster casserole

someday soon if you wish.'

"'Sounds great!'

"It was after weeks of oyster stews, oyster casseroles, raw oysters, chatting and playing cribbage during his afternoon visits, never evenings and never on weekends, that he made his move. I should have realized that either a wife or a girlfriend was in the picture, but by then I would have climbed a rope ladder to the moon for his company. His approach was a comparatively long time in coming, but inevitable.

"'Let's not have another drink. Let's take a nap.'

"I was stunned. 'I thought you'd never ask.'

"'Then I haven't offended you?'

"While he meandered to the bedroom, I sneaked a really heavy shot of inhibition-drowning brandy, which does have a certain amount of indisputable command. Deep down, I was embarrassed and scared. Geez, Cass, he knew tricks that I never knew existed. He ever so slowly manipulated and caressed those areas that brought me to the brink of hysteria, with climaxes of explosive, nerve-shattering intensity, never missing a beat. I gave myself to him totally, Cass, trusting him, believing in him unconditionally and thinking that I was throbbingly in love. Shamelessly, he built my passion and kindled the desires of my devotion.

"I wondered at the time how he could laugh during sex, a new and puzzling experience to me, and chide me, but still flatter my locked-up soul with not even a whispering voice of guilt. He taught me well and flattered me constantly. Sex like that I have never known. Past experiences were like comparing a whistling tea kettle to a pipe organ. And he knew it. I loved his screaming orgasms, never suspecting that that was part of his act. My God, Cass, if sex were a fast food, he would have had an arch over his head. Unfortunately, I chose to ignore the facts and went right on indulging in desires all to end in sickening disgust, lacerations of remorse and self-loathing.

"He must have enjoyed himself, too, Cass, because it took him seven months of fun, fishing, walking on the beach and in the woods, sunning on my deck, and going to singles dances before he made his big pitch. During those fun times, he had shared with me what I thought was real pain in his life. He was in love with someone else, but it was a May-December relationship, and it wasn't working. To me, that meant that there was hope. Unluckily, I didn't know then that that is another ploy of hunters who are avoiding commitment. But what the hell, I was enjoying myself, and all my friends thought that he was a trophy, a great falcon to wear on my wrist.

"Now, after a loss of dollars in five figures, I realize that he had the killer instinct of a rattlesnake. What I thought was a precious diamond was only a cheap piece of glass. But even glass can wound and do a great deal of damage. In all honesty though, I was warned, Cass. He emphasized that it would be strictly business, a loan that would pay off and make some money for both of us. It sounded rational. I wanted some type of interesting work to keep busy, and doing the art work and sales would do it. I did have the presence of mind enough to have my attorney draw up a legal promissory note, very much opposed by my lawyer.

"'What does he have for collateral, Sue?'

"'Nothing!'

"He, according to him, had just lost fifty thousand dollars in another business, but he did not tell me that he was already in debt, which amounted to fraud. It did seem strange that he scrawled his signature and date on the promissory note without even reading it, therefore not complaining about the high interest. Now I know *why*—a con artist. That note might just as well have been kept for wrapping fish. And just as Amy has said, 'The one who turns you on is the one who does you in.'

"And that he did, with no warning. His depth of evasiveness was phenomenal, so I should have suspected something faulty. I hope to hell he is swinging on the knot that I tied at the end of his rope. But then, I probably should try to remember him as a poor old man trying hard to feather his nest, because he certainly will never be the cause for universal mourning. I won't bore you with the details, but fighting his chapter-seven bankruptcy claim was expensive and a real education in the agonizingly slow process of the courts. Jack's lady lawyer even expressed sympathy for my loss, but she was paid, I hope, to do a job and persisted. Thankfully, just one call to my attorneys settled the whole mess in my favor. The product was mine, while his reputation as a deadbeat ran rampant!

"It was apparent that he did not realize that a debt of honor has to be paid or you lose your reputation, that shirking your debt to people who trusted you is morally reprehensible. But there again, it is only the educated man who knows and can properly appraise the consequences of his actions. It is too late for Jack to realize that what determines the measure of a man is the way he handles himself when he is in a situation that he cannot control, that it is a matter of showing grace under pressure. But he certainly knows by now that he who has the money has the clout.

"I must admit that selling the product was fun. I traveled extensively and made many new friends who were willing to help. Strangely enough, some of those had known of Jack's past antics, how he had used the gutter cunning of his species. I made a point of checking out some of Jack's actions of preying upon other individuals.

It was sad hearing the tale of one lady who had lost her impressive lakeside home, to be left living in a trailer park in her little tin house, as she called it. Another had lost her restaurant, and others had had to dun him constantly for unpaid cash loans. He must have been named Jack, short for jackass. Right now, on a scale of one to ten, I would give him a two, but that's because I've never seen a one before. But maybe he wasn't such a jackass after all. He's the one who took the elevator, while I took the shaft. No doubt he has gone about his business and found another victim by now.

"You can bet, Cass, that if another affair slides into my life, he shall have his background checked thoroughly. After that scenario, my promise to myself is that in the future I shall try to love with only one quarter of my heart and give the other three quarters to an available, monogamous playmate. No more parties in the bottom of a booze barrel, where you meet those who should be slithering along the floor, leaving a trail of slime behind them. No more looking for knights on white chargers, who have a way of metamorphosizing into bloated toads. No more turning something white, pure, and beautiful into muddy sludge. No more putting all my eggs into one bastard. The wounds have not healed, and no one will get the chance to open them up again. Dammit, I don't have the courage to trust again, and I hate being cramped with jealousy and resentment. Sounds bitter and cynical as hell, right?"

"That's the mother of all understatements, Sue, but there's no future in our trying to bury our bitterness any longer. We are both tired of falling in and out of love and know that it is a proven process as predictable as the flooding and draining of locks in the Panama Canal. We've both done things with our body that don't have anything to do with our heart or mind and have been damnably sorry a moment later. But we can't continue living on the hard crusts of resignation. Now we both realize and have admitted to each other that what we sowed in folly we reaped in tears. Right now, I'm feeling really scooped out, totally fragmented, so I'll take your advice and make an appointment with your Dr. Amy Fielding."

9

Feeling as though she had just departed an emotional war zone, Cass approached the rambling, white, wedgewood-blue shuttered home, where Dr. Amy Fielding kept her appointments. Cass was put completely at ease when two blue Belton setters greeted her at the door. The doctor wore no white coat. There was no formal office, but a cozy fire burning and a teapot with matching china cups, plus dainty cucumber sandwiches arranged on a nearby table. No wall-to-wall carpeting, but gleaming hardwood floors with brightly colored braided rugs tastefully placed. The dogs promptly settled at Cass's feet. How she ached to have faithful companions like that for her own.

Dr. Amy Fielding was a strikingly handsome woman, very wholesome, and wearing no makeup. Her salt and pepper hair fell attractively to the shoulders of her gray tweed suit. No slacks for this lady, but a severely tailored skirt and sensible walking shoes. Her expressive blue eyes, framed by heavy unplucked eyebrows inadvertently studied Cass; she put her at ease by nodding to her two setters draped about Cass's feet.

"Millie and Nell have certainly taken to you promptly, Cass. They have momentarily deserted me for one whom they innately know truly loves dogs. Do you have any pets?"

"Not yet. I presently have neither the courage nor the stamina to put another down. I have always had cocker spaniels frolicking about, but the last loss was a close call to my physical collapse. Living alone, I have a perfect horror of being hospitalized and having to submit a pet to a kennel. I know from past experience that that is heart-breaking. And besides, I have been traveling fairly extensively."

"You seem to be dealing with some pretty tough traumas, Cass. Sue briefed me a bit. She is a good friend, isn't she. I do hope that I can help. As this doesn't seem to be in the emergency category, do you think that reading your manuscript would help rather than hearing the problems verbally from you right now? I would suggest that you leave it with me so that I might gather whatever insights possible. Then we can try to find some answers."

"That would seem to be the efficient way to handle it, Dr. Fielding."

"Call me Amy, please, Cass. I would like to be a friend as well as a possible advisor. After we become better acquainted, perhaps Sue, you, and I can get together. She seems to have had some struggles comparable to yours, and she trusts you implicitly."

Tears came to Cass's eyes. That word *trust* convinced her that Amy was her next step toward healing. She reached down to pat Nell and Millie, trying to hide her emotions.

"I would like that, Amy. Thank you for giving me your time, and I will wait to hear from you. It is so peaceful and comfortable here that I hate to leave, but I must."

Amy accompanied her to the car, with the dogs winding around their legs. How she hated to leave there and go home with no one to greet her, although she seemed to be carrying Amy's aura of serenity with her. She was already looking forward to her next visit.

When her own driveway came into view, Cass was exhilarated—the clan had gathered. There was Sybil's silver Volvo, Pat's cardinal red Cougar, so Schultzie would be there, too, Enid's gold Mercedes, and Sue's sleek Biarritz. Friends are treasures, and Cass could count them all on one hand. Before switching off the engine, she could hear Schultzie, Pat's excitable, tiny Yorkie, barking his greeting. Cass loved him, and he knew it. The delicate little head with shiny expressive eyes appeared just barely over the bottom of the screen door. He knew that she was home and greeted her with midair flips and delighted yips. As soon as Cass dropped her purse, Schultzie leaped into her arms, cuddling and mewling, almost as though he knew that his buddy needed cheering.

All of her cohorts, sporting tans and in various attire, were lounging about on the sundeck. Misty-eyed, Cass thought, *What a blessing to have them here, unannounced, just* here, *as they always were in many ways!*

"Hey, thanks for being here, gals. Gawd, what a prosperous looking dooryard. Yup, we're all here, but the big question is are we all there."

They knew where she had been but languidly sipped their tall icy drinks, waiting for her to talk when she was ready.

Finally, Enid, in her flowing mu-mu from Hawaii, was the first to leave her chaise.

"We're way ahead of you, Cass, let me build you one. And yes, I know you miss CeeCee and so does Schultzie. But don't panic, she's just being groomed. The vet will deliver her here later. Hopefully one of us will be sober enough to get the door when they arrive."

"When I didn't see that wee little white face at the door with Schultzie, my heart did lurch, Enid. But I'm edgy as hell anyway, and as long as she's okay, let's do some serious sipping. But first, do we need food, or shall I go out and kill something?"

"You know better than that, Cass. The fridge is full of finger food plus some things we can nuke a little later," Pat sputtered, her drinking arm raised like a pitcher's throw. "I even brought the microwave, knowing that you refuse to own one, and everyone knows that's because you expect your next enterprise might have a pacemaker." That was a private joke among the five of them, and Pat would never let Cass forget her chance excuse many months ago.

Pat was always the one to remember the food and never came to any of their gatherings without everyone's favorite dips, munchies, salads, and casseroles. She was the domestic one of the group and loved to spoil people with her gourmet preparations.

Sybil's exuberant personality was the next to burst.

"Okay, kid, what was it like? To hell with being polite and creeping around on egg shells. Did you tell her about your son? I will probably be Amy's next client anyway. I'm sick of being in tears over my escapades and swearing off the entire male gender every other month or so." Sybil had just returned from an extensive cruise, taken only to get over a passion that had waned, sputtered, flared, and died, like a campfire in a drizzle. "Can she handle straight talk, Cass? I'm convinced that it would be far easier to talk to a gal, but you know how I tell it like it is in some pretty powerful language that isn't accepted by everyone.

"Without embarrassing her, could I tell her that this last sunnuvabitch confused his mind with his penis, which is understandable, as they are both pretty pathetic. But I still went squirrely, didn't I? Geez, when I think back, the prick would show up for the weekend with one shirt and a ten-dollar bill and never changed either one. Everyone to whom I introduced him measured his class on a minus scale, even you guys. And you all know how important a man's clothes are to me. That wimp didn't know peau de soir from canvas. I'll be damned if I know why I still miss him. It must be the scotch-illumined paradise that I live in. Do you think Amy would even consider helping me pick up the litter of my life and make a success out of something? Christ, I'm sick of walking around with a cup full of anger and trying not to spill it."

Up to this point, Enid had not said a word but was getting a bit foxed along with the rest. Wearing enough jewelry to anchor a fair-sized yacht and with hands on her hips, she expounded.

"To hell with all the wham-bams, the wonder minks. As far as I'm concerned, they've all had cement jobs performed on their hearts, and what we all need are bullshit protectors. I betcha Amy would say the same, no doubt caged in a little different vernacular. My last one should have been hit by lightning to weld his fly shut. All of you met him the night you were out trolling through the bars at the beach. Remember, he didn't even buy you a drink? He didn't even offer, but he was tighter than an ant's ass anyway.

"Forgive me for raving, gals, I guess I must be having one of those days. Cripes, I'm beginning to think I'm having one of those *lives!* But it just can't be the end of the *nui nui*. In Hawaii that's a rainbow to you slip sailors. Why don't we eat, drink, screw, and otherwise be merry the whole rest of our lives. Gotta freshen my drink, then it's someone else's turn to expound on the goddam Don Juans who seem to be the bane of our existence."

Pat had taken the dogs down to the lawn for exercise, but had heard all the chatter from above. She was the lone member of the clan who had been smart enough to survive being a clay pigeon. Even though she had been a target, she was still all in one piece. Chuckling, then breaking into a deep belly laugh, she looked up at Cass, whose long, shapely legs were draped over the railing.

"Cass, remember the lily-pad hopper that you tagged Step-and-a-half? You never could figure out why I didn't know why he limped. And that night at Singles was a hoot when he was down in the darkest corner swapping spit with that one who looked like a slut in a grade-B movie. You went down to say hi and rapped him on the back of his head so hard that his front teeth chipped. Then how about the nerd who always complained about jet lag when he had only flown in from Chicago. He thought he was a real winner until your spaniel snatched off his hair piece. That scenario should have been on video tape." At that point, Pat returned to the deck and flopped.

"Really, all of you will be able to laugh at your encounters one day. Oh, and Cass, recall the all-American boy who was hooked on music, a college classmate of mine? Gawd, he always wore a cape. The day we visited his home, I nearly went ballistic when you asked him why in the hell he had a hole cut in the floor of his den. He put up his erector-set type music rack and explained that was his podium when fantasizing being the director of a symphony orchestra. We never did figure out why the podium was lowered, not raised. It was a wonder we didn't go off the road driving home, utterly gasping with glee. Maybe we should go back some day." All this had happened before the present clan had become so close. Cass recovered her breath.

"Right, Pat, most of your affairs did radiate humor, somehow, but you went through literal hell with me after Rex left. Those marathon phone calls kept me perking many, many times. And you were always available to take a ride somewhere. That night at the bar, during a liquor salesmen's convention neither of us will forget, I'm certain, you spotted that dinner-jacketed phony long before I did. When he followed us out to the car, you kept muttering 'arrivederci,' and I wondered how in the hell you knew his name was Harry Daverchy. So much for the potent drinks at that bar. I remember it all, Pat, like it was yesterday. You have stuck by me for many years, dark, light, thick, and thin. Do you really think the day will ever come when I will shut the door and relish having the privacy of my home, alone, knowing that I don't need a male to lean on?"

"If we're not leaning, we won't fall, Cass. You'll all get there, I promise. Perhaps Amy will convince you of that, but it does take time. Just try not to get *involved*. Find a companion that does not in any way invoke jealousy, *couldn't* in any way. Hopefully, you won't get smart too late.

"My current companion, Tim, has been very helpful, although it took a while to overcome his seemingly haughty disdain for such social imperatives as cleanliness. His aversion to soap and water, Efferdent and Listerine leaned toward a questionable friendship in the beginning. But with persistence and lots of fingernail-soaking in Clorox, I won that battle, because he is kind, sincere, thoughtful, and willing to go anywhere and do anything at any time. That at least keeps me in circulation, and who knows whether I might meet someone else. I'm not looking for Mr. Right but Mr. Right Now!

"When you meet Tim, you will tell me, I know, that he has the personality of a pig on Valium, that he is grossly corpulent, and bald, too, but if I wanted hair, I'd adopt a monkey. So there again, it's an easy friendship, no jealousy, no hanging up the phone waiting for it to ring, and no pressure. He also has many other friends, so I don't run a guilt trip when I choose to be elsewhere. That means something, doesn't it? That's what I mean by avoiding becoming involved."

Sue had half-heartedly listened to it all and finally interrupted.

"Keeriste, Pat, you sound as though you are right up there with Plato and Aristotle. And with that description of Tim, you must be on an extended sex sabbatical, too. But maybe I should look for that type. I'm so sick of living my life like a Greek tragedy, but Amy *is* helping. When I first went to her office, I was racing downhill like a free-wheeling locomotive going downgrade without any brakes. At the rate I was going, my future would have lasted about a week. I am praying and feel secure that Amy is going to help you, too, Cass. Then, just maybe, she will be agreeable to group therapy for all of us. But hey, life is to be enjoyed, not endured, so let's have a bite to eat, then go rattle a few cages."

10

Cass had told the clan that (a), she was favorably impressed with Amy, (b), Amy was reading the manuscript re her life before any diagnostic sessions, and (c), she would keep them all informed. It had been four days since meeting Amy, and it seemed a lifetime. The phone rang.

"Cass, this is Amy Fielding. Were you beginning to think that I had forgotten you? How are you?"

"Fine, thanks, and just pacing, waiting to hear from you. Did the material that I left give you any insight into where I should go from here?"

"Indeed, Cass, it is appalling, and I do very much want to do my best to assist. Are you available tomorrow after lunch, let's say one o'clock?"

"I'll definitely be there, Amy, and thanks for calling."

Cass was greeted with jumps and bounds by Millie and Nell when Amy opened the door. She had brought squeak toys for them both and played with them briefly.

"I do so appreciate your going through that material, Amy. Now I will truly listen carefully and am ready to accept all comments whether negative, positive, or both."

"Fine, then if you don't object, I would like to tape our conversations. In that way I will be able to furnish you with a printout to review at home. As a result, you may be aware of subjects that you did not intend to omit. Also, it will be easier for you to review, or further question, any suggestions I have made, which you may want to discuss in more detail later.

"Having studied your background and past experiences, Cass, it is my firm opinion that we must come to some solution about your son, Archer. That is heart-wrenching and will prey on your mind forever. There are ways of tracing blood relatives, and I can put the operation into effect, saving you from suffering through the legalities and investigations. I can do all that for you, then proceed with whatever information is available. It has been proven that in many cases, the child searches for his parents, and we must find the reason why he has not done that. Or perhaps he did try and was not successful. You have moved about a bit, Cass, but having known you this short time, I am convinced that he would love you deeply. Do you feel that I should proceed? I do strongly advise it."

"You have no idea the number of times I have fantasized about this very thing, Amy, but I don't want to hurt anyone else. What might the results do to those who adopted him if they are still alive? What effect would a shock of this sort have on Archer? What effect would it have on his wife and children, if any?"

"How do we know that he was adopted? How do we know that he is happy or, for that matter, even alive? There are many other facets to this type of problem, but before we make an actual commitment to move, we will attend a few sessions with a clinical psychologist and take it from there. When we find Archer, he may have physical or mental defects that might be difficult for you to deal with. Are you prepared to face a heartbreak like that?"

Cass gave a prolonged, tearful, and whimpering sigh.

"That would be better than always wondering and never knowing, and I will always love him, whatever his condition. Of that I am certain, so let's do it. Let me give you whatever information that I have for a start. It's all here in print and documented."

"I shall make that my prime objective, Cass, but meanwhile I think we should chat. Until this is resolved, I might suggest that self-discipline is what you need. Of that, I am certain. Recall that kindness and faith worked wonders during your years in the teaching field. Control was the result. Now try a little kindness and faith in yourself, Cass. Don't depend upon others to fill the voids in your life, but try being a friend to yourself. Remember that you are intelligent, compassionate, honest, loyal, and sincere. Why aren't you all of these to yourself? Why do you wait and wait and wait for someone else to tell you that. You do *not* need their approbation. You already know that. Slow down, relax, and realize that *you* are your own best friend.

"You have tried cathecting. Did it work for you? No. It resulted in pain, wasted hours of letting your brilliant mind meander, resulting in promises to yourself, which were promptly forgotten when the current suitor knocked on the door. Why do you allow those short circuits to interrupt the peace and serenity that you deserve? You know well those who need diamonds, platinum, and gold. You do not. You have them. Neither do you need brass, lead, or zinc. Your inner being calls for much more than elements. You need the ever-elusive balance of the cosmos, the balanced scale of physical, mental, and emotional well-being.

"Take time to ponder your hours of idle chatter, your abhorrence of most dialogues of the deaf. It is too late to regret the time spent involved in such a waste. Think back on the body language of those desperate people trying to convince someone of something, the forced laughter, the shrill pitch of feminine voices, the bored guffaws of male presence, and the end result, nothing. Unless perhaps there were repercussions of jealous, idle gossip. Were you not often the target of that? It hurt, didn't it? But when you took the time, if you bothered to analyze the situation, *you knew*. You knew that one who is, in appearance at least, in control of her life is often the target of desperately lonely, jealous females and the male contingent whose past advances had been frustrated. Dwell on that, and mindfully accent the peace of your independent existence.

"I have used the word, existence, Cass, but it is much more than that in your circumstances. You do not need the party-boy type of companion. You've had that. It seemed fun at the time, didn't it! And possibly it was, but you have grown. Most of your acquaintances are still pursuing the facade of 'social togetherness.' You do not need it, as you have been there and, hopefully, now realize that it's a matter of escape, and that is why you do not care. It is a time-consuming rat race, particularly when most do not take the time to ponder whether they are running *from* one or *to* another enterprise.

"Be thankful, Cass, that you have had the good fortune of an adoring husband, a fulfilling sex life, the broadening experience of world travel, and mostly, the understanding and lasting friendship of both males and females who admire your lifestyle now that you are alone.

"Try to understand and plumb the depths of your empathy for those who are still running. To some, it is of major importance to have closets full of clothes, ready for all occasions, and willing to don them when given a last-minute invitation. Seemingly, the companion makes little difference, as long as there is exposure. They fill their days with a special emptiness, made up of social vendettas, hypochondria, cocktail parties, adventures in pseudo culture, random fornications, and semialcoholism. And when it gets so dull that even they become aware of it, they take all their frantic aimlessness to St. Thomas, Nassau, Jamaica, etcetera, and brag about their hangovers when they return. And it is a fact, percentage-wise, there are many more females than males in this category. Be that as it may, Cass, other than the agonizing mystery of your son, Archer, what do you think is hurting the most right now?"

"Amy, it's brutally lonely when you have the feeling that you have been disowned by your entire family, for no apparent reason. In retrospect, it is my firm belief that my total life has been sharing, to the extent that my efforts resulted in total loss, materially, emotionally, physically, and economically.

"During preteens and throughout high school, the hand-me-downs were gratefully accepted. There was no question that feeding and clothing four kids shortly after the depression was an economic problem for my parents, a fact of life. To me, it really was no problem as long as books were available. I didn't learn until much later that throughout history the third child or the middle child seems to be the underdog.

"It is not strange that in my teen years, my friends were just there, taken for granted? But not so in later life. Luckily I can count them on one hand, but family is family. 'Blood is thicker' and all that stuff. Maybe it isn't. Is it a possibility that sentiment has overcome rational reasoning? I tried to talk myself into believing that old adage, but it didn't work.

"Have I been too certain that the rose-colored glasses would never break or be stolen, that the carpet would always be there, never pulled out from under me, that the vows I took would always and forever be upheld, never be broken, that the trust I had would never have reason to turn me to cynicism?

"How do you hold on? try one more time? believe in the seven times seven rhetoric? go one more mile? I could not expect my friends to be supportive when negativity seemed to reign. Do you suppose that I have taken too much for granted during my entire life? Have I expected too much of myself and everyone else? Did I deeply appreciate the good life but make the mistake of not showing it to anyone? That must be a definite probability, Amy. What do you think?"

"Cass, it is definitely time to slow down and take stock, to start studying your sense of values and to search for what is within. Try evaluating your acquaintances. Did they appear on your doorstep because they enjoyed your company? Or was it a hangout during their spare time?"

"But I find it easier when I have people around, Amy. It helps to forget for the moment. It also seems that when they leave, in the quietude following, I seem to realize most that friends do fill part of the void. But when I have shared my home and my thoughts and have freely given my love and compassion, Amy, I have given it all. Why try to continue? There is no more to give."

"It seems that reality has finally seeped in, Cass. In fact, didn't the door slam on the realization that it has been a one-way street? Did any true sharing occur? Too much subterfuge has taken place, and again you have trusted too many with too much too often. You put yourself up as a real mark, a true *clay pigeon*."

"That is right on target, Amy. I am on the verge of crawling back into my cocoon to avoid coping with any more battered emotions resulting from associations with men. I am struggling through construction rather than driving into a chasm. Having been a casualty twice is enough. It would be devastating trying to emerge from the chrysalis alone, so, hopefully, I can stay in it with a minimum of outside contact. When I feel strong enough to emerge, I shall be much more cautious with my male associations. At present, I'd like to throw them all into an oven and nuke them."

"That is a start, Cass. A woman can be pushed only

so far before she takes steps to remove an irritant from her life. At least, you are willing to admit to your wrong choices. Earlier in life, you were obviously surrounded by people who were generous, friendly, and genuinely fond of you and you thought the entire human race was cast in the same mold. Now, hopefully, you are on the track of finding a way to face yourself, to learn to live with yourself, and be patient with yourself. Would you give your credit card to a comparative stranger and expect him to use it for your own good always? Why place your trust and contentment on the back of someone and expect him to handle it with care?

"It is sad that when dealing with some, one has to pick and choose to find the truth. It is astounding the abuse and hurt and ugliness that human beings inflict on one another. As I have reviewed with Sue, there are many out there who are very shrewd in small matters, like taking advantage, getting the best of the bargain, seeking the finest opportunity to cheat, but are hopelessly illogical in larger affairs, as the peasant mind always is. But on the principle that there is always someone worse off than yourself, realizing it may be the first step in contentedness. At this point, I believe my first suggestion, when you do venture out into the circuit, is to watch out for those who make a grotesque mockery out of being a confidant."

"As you know, I have already made that mistake, but your advice will accent my avoidance of that type forevermore."

"That's understandable, Cass. Now let's see if we can illuminate the cave in which you are hiding, unlock the door you have closed against future happiness. An emancipated woman is one who recognizes her needs and fulfills them, so let's continue to review some of the pitfalls in this effort. This brings to my mind the advice given to a wife by a mistress, 'Don't let your happiness depend on someone else.' Don't try so hard to please. Go about your business and be done with it. Be courteous, but don't sacrifice your inner integrity by asking for anyone's approval."

"That does seem to be what I have been doing, Amy, but now with more hope in my heart about Archer, I will be much, much stronger, now that I have something solid to look forward to."

"You must remember that we cannot be certain that all we uncover from our investigation will be good news. I assure you that whatever the end results are, it will be healthier for your future stability to know the truth. I will always be here to help you through the rough times. While we're waiting for some answers, I think that our next session should be based on recognizing the womanizer types that are out there. Try to relax, and before our next meeting make a note of any definite questions that you may want to discuss. Is next Tuesday at this same time convenient for you?"

"I shall be looking forward to it, Amy. And if you ever need a dog-sitter, may I be on your list?"

11

The next visit was one that Cass was very thankful to have in print.

"Cass, our Archer project is in the works. Of course, it is too early for any news as yet, but at least I can promise you that we have made a move that is definitely in the right direction. Now unless you have some questions, I want to share with you what knowledge I do have regarding the womanizer types in our midst.

"Basically, theirs is the thrill of the hunt. They have to score. (Strangely enough, isn't 'score' the word used in tallying when competing in skeet shooting with clay pigeons as the targets?) Then their interest fades, and they are on the move again. The Don Juan's appeal is that he makes you feel as if he had finally found his soul mate. The fascination he exerts is the erotic interest he expresses, and that seems to have universal appeal. As Sue's friends so succinctly expressed it, 'Jack was a trophy to wear like a falcon on her wrist.'

"Most psychiatrists agree that the fear of long-term intimacy is one trait that distinguishes the Don Juan. They invariably avoid permanent relationships. As soon as they come too close, they develop a phobia, a trapped feeling. For them the only safety is in numbers.

"Haven't you noticed that they need constant admiration? Didn't you consider them conceited? They are not so much interested in you as a woman as they are in your response to them. Was it, not 'I love you,' but 'I need you'; quite different. They work very hard at the game of seduction and know how to pluck just the right strings.

"You've had to sort through the wreckage of your affairs. You were naive and inexperienced with this type, so were badly hurt, but one can rebound. Just try to remember that when a Don Juan asks you to dance, join him for a set if you wish, just don't expect to be his partner for long. Unfortunately, because of the trend of permissiveness, which has been devastating to society, he no longer must leap social and moral barriers to reach his prey. His erotic meanderings do not call for stern condemnations anymore, and he is very much aware of it. This is all the more reason that we must be aware of his antics and constantly remind ourselves that the typical womanizer is psychologically incapable of a sincere and honest, monogamous relationship with a woman. Never forget this. And it is on record that if one thinks that she can tame the Don Juan, she is on an impossible ego trip.

"Cass, at the risk of redundancy, I must repeat, in order to impress upon you, that one can rebound from such affairs. If you sort through the wreckage, you will never again become a victim. At the time, you were weak and indecisive. You broke up and got back together an embarrassing number of times until now you are so miserable that you have decided to make a complete split from that yo-yo existence.

"You will have no trouble with this, Cass. I'm certain that you are much too busy to spend time reading romantic novels, which are nothing more than a fantasy of what life may be like with a beloved. If reading is an escape for you, it is far better to read persuasive writers who can be put on record as knowing that romantic love is a scourge, a murderous game of emotions, and protracted torture. I can refer you to many books on this subject if you feel they would help.

"You have already experienced what drinking will do

to you. You sought solace in liquor and found that it was disastrous in handling loneliness and heartbreak, right? In fact, you have already put into practice most of the methods of pushing unhappy-in-love affairs behind you, such as (a) you have dwelled on his negative points, (b) you have provided for yourself all the little extras that he brought as incentives, and (c) you learned to stay away from all reminders of him, whether it was movies, people, or places! Most important of all, Cass, you have loyal friends who are trying to draw you back into a rewarding social life, because they know that you have not totally buried your basically healthy urge to enjoy life."

"I realize that I can't let down my supportive friends now, Amy. I just want no more of the turbulence, just tranquillity. There simply isn't any future in digging into the past other than trying to settle once and for all what has happened to Archer. Some of my self-confidence has been restored, since I have placed no value or consideration higher than reality and no concern higher than to respect the facts."

"It is refreshing that you are aware of all this, Cass. You have defeated some of the hurdles of dwelling over the beautiful past and forgetting most of the physically and emotionally damaging situations. I know now that you realize it is unbearably dangerous to invest so much emotional capital in another human being, unless we find Archer."

12

It was disappointing, a super letdown, when Amy left a message canceling the Tuesday appointment. Cass returned the call to find that Amy had to be out of town. Due to an emergency, all appointments were canceled until further notice. Was she ill? Was she personally searching for Archer? Who was caring for Nell and Millie? Did they go with her? Cass's imagination ran amok. Couldn't she have been of some assistance? Did Sue know what had happened? Call Sue... Not home, dammit.

Cass had absorbed too many positive ideas to put everything out of her mind even for a few hours. Thankfully, she could review Amy's notes. She had been deeply impressed with the discussion of the difference between love and infatuation. She knew now that she had spent too much time searching for relationships to consider the obvious differences. According to the stats, her experiences had been infatuations. Hadn't she been eager and excited, but really not happy? In each relationship, hadn't she had nagging doubts that she had not dared examine too closely? Hadn't she always carried feelings of insecurity? Hadn't she lacked confidence, always wondering whether the significant one was cheating? Hadn't she checked on their whereabouts and done other things that she regretted? Yes to all of these, which roughly hinted at infatuation.

Had there been trust? Had she felt secure and unthreatened? Had she taken the time to become friends before becoming lovers? Had she gained strength and quiet understanding and acceptance of their imperfections? No to all of these that would have defined love; they seemed to be the clinchers. She had not known love! It all had been infatuations. Amy would be encouraged to know that Cass recognized and was not ashamed to admit all this.

Call Sue again! Finally, she was answering. She had received the same message, of course, and had no clue to Amy's whereabouts. They would just have to remain in the wait-and-see mode.

"Sue, how long have you known Amy? I know that she has top-notch professional credentials, but what about her personal life? Had she ever been married? Did she have any children? Has she always lived in this area?"

"Yes, she is a New Englander and was married at one time to an attorney. She has spoken very little of him, but people who knew him spoke of his being hot tempered and abusive. As Amy has admitted, she should have known something was amiss when she discovered that she was his third living wife. He also had a son who had very little to do with his father. I do know that the divorce was not that devastating to Amy, but she and her stepson had become very fond of each other. If I recall correctly, her ex-husband is dead and her stepson was in the military. I have no idea what branch or where or whether they still keep in touch. For her sake, I certainly hope that there is no problem there."

Cass had driven by Amy's home innumerable times, hoping that she might have returned and had not had the time to resume her schedule. But there was no activity. For five long weeks, Cass had hoped and prayed that there would be some contact soon. After all, she, reasoned, they were not close friends as yet, and why should Amy be sharing her problems with Cass. Surely, she had many friends and, presumably, relatives somewhere. But this was an emergency, and to Cass, that meant trouble of some kind.

Like a bolt out of the blue, Amy surfaced. When she called, it was with the assurance that she was fine though humbly apologetic for her abrupt cancellation. Could Cass come for lunch on the next Tuesday? "Come early and let's chat."

Tuesday seemed like eons of waiting. When Cass drove into the now familiar drive, Millie and Nell were already outside, bounding and leaping with joy at the sight of Cass. They remembered her. Hearing the din of the reunion, Amy came outside to greet her as well.

"Do come in, Cass, we have lunch all ready for you."

"We?" Cass muttered, thoroughly puzzled, which was totally ignored. Amy was bubbling with chatter as Cass followed her to the sun room, with its bright yellow wicker furniture, the table covered with a lemon yellow table cloth and a centerpiece of fresh, dewey daffodils. Sitting at the table was the handsomest child Cass had ever seen. She devoured his looks in one glance—flashing eyes like blue topaz, crisply, curling black hair, fair skin, and gleaming white teeth as he smiled and offered his hand in greeting.

"Hi, Cass, I'm Chad Fielding. I've been looking forward to meeting you, and Nana Amy said it would be okay to call you Cass. Is it okay?" Millie and Nell had arranged themselves on each side of Chad, still breathless and panting.

"Of course, Chad, and I'm very happy to meet you. But you will have to forgive me if I appear a little jealous of the attention Millie and Nell are giving you. I have become very fond of them."

"I'll share them, Cass; pretty cool, aren't they. I've never had a dog before because I had to move so much.

Do you like pizza? That's what we're having, and ice cream, too."

Cass felt as though she had known this appealing child forever but was puzzled that he did not attempt to leave the table, as most children, in her experience, were prone to do. It was almost as though Chad had sensed her puzzlement.

"You are very pretty, and I like you, just as Nana Amy said I would. I want very much to get up and give you a hug, but it's hard to do. I'm a cripple, but you won't notice it after awhile. Please don't be shocked."

Dear God, the child had braces on both legs, which she had not seen, as the table cloth covered them. Fighting harder than at any time in her life to hold back tears, she quickly moved to give him a bear hug.

"Chad, how brave you are! And now I'm so happy to have three new friends to play with, you, Nell, and Millie."

Amy had disappeared into the kitchen to totally lose it. She was shaken with emotion over Chad's acceptance of his handicap and his adult manner of showing hospitality to a total stranger. When she returned, her eyes suspiciously red, she served lunch followed by Chad's favorite dessert, vanilla ice cream smothered with fresh strawberries.

"Oh, wow, Nana, I hope there are seconds. You're not allergic to strawberries, are you, Cass? Lots of people are, you know. Nana, I was just telling Cass about the plane crash, but we can tell her more about it later. Gosh, I'm glad you're here. You have pretty eyes like my dad's. His were blue, too. Do you live very far from here? Do you have any pets? I know you don't have any children 'cause, Nana, Amy already told me that. I need lots of new friends, and I hope you'll be one of them, will you?" All this was with the machine-gun chatter of a ten-year-old.

"I guess I need new relatives, too. Mom and Dad have gone to their condo in the sky, and I don't even remember my grandparents. Even though Nana Amy is my grandma now, I could sure use two. Maybe you don't want to be a grandma 'cause some people think it sounds old, don't they." Still a steady stream of chatter, never stopping for an answer, but closely watching Cass's facial expressions.
"Nana Amy, could I tell Cass about the accident?"
"Of course, Chad. I can fill her in on the details later."
"Well, my dad was a doctor. He told me I could be anything I want to be 'cause his dad, my grandpa, wanted Dad to be a lawyer, and I guess they fought over that. But anyway, my mom, Jill, was a nurse, and that's why they wanted to work at a place called American Lake in the state of Washington. It is a Veterans Hospital, where they wanted to do some good, they said. Mom told me a lot about it while we were waiting for Dad to come home from Hanoi. He was over there with some very important people from Washington, D.C. That's where the president lives, not where the hospital is.

"Those men that Dad traveled to Hanoi with were trying to get back our prisoners of war. Dad was over there a long time himself in a place called Danang. He told me about some of it, but he was funny, saying that lots of the time, he lived like a possum, 'cause his medical station was underground. Isn't that crazy? Dad was over there three years before I was born, but this time it was only two weeks. Mom and I missed him something awful and couldn't wait to meet him in Seattle when he came back. If I'm talking too fast, please tell me. Gosh, I miss 'em, but at least they didn't see me like this. Or maybe they can, do you think so?"

"I'm sure they are your guardian angels, Chad, and that they are very proud of how brave you are." Cass offered, again fighting to hold back tears.

"Well, it helps to talk about it. But I'm still kinda mixed up about what happened after the plane crash. You see, Mom and I flew from Boston and met Dad in Seattle. Gosh, it's pretty there, and I wanted to go back. We visited that hospital that I told you about, and we were coming back to Boston to move everything out there, you know, sell our house and everything. Mom and Dad laughed a lot about the end of a million-dollar surgeon's career, but I didn't understand that. I wanted to move there really bad, too, 'cause Dad explained how close we would be to Alaska, and that's where I'm going to live and have my own plane, too. Did you know that when kids in Alaska have birthday parties, their dads fly them from one to another in planes? Everyone has to have a plane, I guess. That's wicked cool, huh?"

"How very strange, Chad. That is one place that I plan to visit again."

"*You* have been there?"

"Oh, yes, and I shall return. Perhaps we can go together some day. You would love the camping, salmon fishing, mammoth glaciers, sled dogs, grizzly bears, caribou, Dall sheep, bald eagles, sea otters, seals, the friendly faces of beluga whales, and the natives, too." Chad was totally entranced, his eyes seemingly as big as ferris wheels. "We'll camp at the foot of Mt. McKinley, North America's highest mountain. That's in the wild Denali National Park. Its beauty is breathtaking I'll show you my slides someday soon. Also, I have a recent copy of *The Milepost,* a travel guide to Alaska, which you can read."

"Did you fly up there, Cass?"

"No, Chad, I drove the Alaska Highway and toured the state in a motor home. There are many miles where there are no roads, but we traveled everywhere that we could. I did fly from Fairbanks to Nome with a bush pilot, though."

"Was he your husband?"

"No, my husband stayed with the motor home, because we had a cocker spaniel with us, and he chose to stay and care for the dog."

"Where is he now?"

"Oh, my husband has gone to his condo in the sky, too, along with our spaniel."

"Were they killed in an accident?"

"No, my husband died of a long illness, and the pup of old age. So you see I'm alone, too. But do you feel like telling me more about the plane crash?"

"Well, I'm not afraid to fly again, but I was wicked scared. It was at night, and I couldn't see anything. I'd been asleep, but I can remember Dad checking my seat belt then telling Mom and me to put our heads down. And then there was a loud crash and lots of screaming and lots of fire. That's all I remember until I woke up in a hospital and Nana Amy was there. Gosh, I had only seen her a few times before, but I was wicked glad to see her. I guess she'll have to tell you the rest, about the men in the funny red hats that helped us out so much. One of them was a friend of Dad's. They are called Shriners. Do you know any of them?"

Amy had escaped to the kitchen again, but returned with steaming cups of cocoa with floating marshmallows.

"Isn't he courageous, Cass? I'm so very thankful that Chad's dad had carried my name and address in his identification papers. And now you know why I had to break our appointment so abruptly so many weeks ago. It has been a very busy time for Chad and me. Now Nell and Millie are coaxing to go outside, so let's take our cocoa and join them."

Chad was an independent youngster and wanted no help in getting about with his braces and crutches. In fact, he made a joke of "hanging ten" in his wheel chair and warned the dogs of his right-of-way rules. It was approaching late afternoon, and everyone was emotionally drained. As casually as possible, Cass made her exit with promises to return soon and assurances that if Chad got lonely during Amy's office hours, she would look forward to his phone calls.

13

The following evening Chad did call.

"Guess what, Cass, Nana Amy and I spent about all day at school, and I'm going to start tomorrow. But they said I'd need a tutor when I go back to Springfield to the Shriners Hospital. Aren't you a teacher? Couldn't you be my tutor? It's only third grade, and the Shriners will even have a place for you to stay in Springfield, and then you could meet Dr. Hamilton, too, and then you'd have another friend, okay?"

"Whoa, slow down, Chad. That sounds great, and of course I'll do it, if approved. I'm properly certified, so there's no problem there. Is Nana Amy available to come to the phone?"

"Cass, we're moving pretty fast, but I do want to discuss all this with you. And I haven't forgotten the investigation re Archer that I'm doing on your part. Can you come over tomorrow while Chad is in school? Come for lunch about eleven, okay?"

"I'll be there, Amy, and thanks."

Lunch was informal, served under the watchful and hopeful eyes of Nell and Millie.

"Cass, I haven't contacted my source re your case since all this has happened, but I shall do so very soon. Are you really available as Chad's tutor once we are informed of the program at the hospital? He would love it, and something like this may be just what you need—great therapy!"

"Yes, yes, I'm available, and I look forward to it."

"While we have the chance, let me give you some brief background on Chad's situation. Chad's dad was named

Todd Fielding by the man who adopted him, Arnold Fielding, my ex-husband. Arnold and his first wife adopted Todd at birth. When Todd was nearly two years old, there was a divorce with his father gaining custody. Within a year, there was a second marriage, and that one lasted only three years, again ending in divorce with Arnold gaining custody again. Being a lawyer gave him a lot of clout. If only I had known all this before I married him.

"Nevertheless, our marriage lasted a record number of years, during which I became very, very fond of Todd, Chad's father. In fact I remained in the marriage longer than I wanted to, but remained for Todd's sake. I was the only mother that Todd had really known. His father, Arnold, never married again after our divorce. He is now deceased; he left Todd with only his wife, Jill, and son, Chad. Thankfully we kept in touch throughout the years, and that is why Chad's dad, Todd, kept my name with his identification.

"During Todd's college years, he attempted to trace his biological parents. He was successful to a degree, but backed off rather than upset the life of his adoptive mother, who at the time had a successful and strong marriage. Todd was a compassionate and caring person who would never hurt anyone intentionally, so he dropped the investigation right there rather than cause any conflict, especially with his father, Arnold, who was adamantly opposed to Todd's tracing his biological parents.

"Todd's marriage to Jill was an ideal union, and Todd was ecstatic when Chad was born. The three of them were inseparable until his investigative trip to Hanoi for the U.S. Government.

"As Chad told you, the ill-fated flight crashed west of Boston on the approach to Logan Airport. Todd and Jill were identified among the victims, but thankfully, Chad was one of the survivors. The officials called Lane Hamilton, a close friend of the family who lives in the outskirts of Boston. He is a Shriner from Aleppo Temple and had Chad immediately flown to the Shriners Hospital for Crippled Children in Springfield, Massachusetts. Lane is a director there and also on the hospital staff. How very lucky Chad is.

"Lane Hamilton called me and met me at the hospital when I left here so suddenly. He has been so efficient with handling everything, arranging the double funeral, and contacting attorneys, which resulted in my being named as legal guardian because Chad has no other living relatives. All that time, I had been staying at quarters supplied by the Shriners for the closest relatives of the patient's family. That is probably where you'll be staying when you tutor Chad while he is hospitalized.

"Lane supervised Chad's diagnosis and participated in all operations, as he is an osteopathic surgeon himself. Springfield is where Chad will be for many weeks to come. I never could have accomplished all this alone. Lane is a widower and has taken Chad's welfare as his special project. He knows that I adored Todd and that Chad will never want for anything as long as he is in my care. I am so thankful that he is as close as Springfield until he is fully healed. The medical team has assured us that one day he will walk as normally as the rest of us. And all of these operations and the therapy is free, Cass. I wonder whether the Shriners get all the credit they deserve. Lane should be calling soon to let me know when to take Chad back to the hospital. I will let you know promptly."

The following Saturday, Amy called to invite Cass for dinner.

"Nothing special, but Chad is anxious to see you, and Lane Hamilton will be here. Now, don't cower because he is of the male gender. He is not on the prowl by any means, but we will be working with him at the hospital, so why not meet him now."

"I'll be there, Amy, and I'll bring the dessert, Chad's favorite, okay?"

"Great, wear slacks, and be comfortable. We may take Chad and the dogs to the park after dinner."

Cass had no qualms about meeting Lane. In fact, as far as she was concerned, he was just part of Chad's recovery, so she dressed in jeans and a blue bulky-knit sweater that matched the color of her eyes. She knew that blue was Chad's favorite color, too. She had made up her mind that of course she would tutor Chad and, hopefully, it would bring her back into being productively involved in life. She had a focus now—Chad's total recovery. No more just keeping busy, schlumping as she called it. No more need for diversions. She now had a goal in life. But Cass silently vowed that she would never give up her search for information about Archer.

Chad, Nell, and Millie were waiting for her on the front lawn. The greeting was riotous, with lots of bouncing, yips, and hugs. She placed the foil-wrapped dessert on Chad's knees.

"Can you handle that while I get my purse?"

"You betcha, Cass, can I peek?" He spun the wheel chair around and headed for the ramp.

"Nope, it's a surprise, and it's not squeezable, so take care. You are in complete charge or no dessert, right? I will be right behind you as soon as I get Nell and Millie's new squeak toys. And I have some toys for you, Nana Amy, Lane, and me, too! But I'll hide those until after dinner."

She was fumbling in the trunk up to her shoulders, reaching for the bag of toys.

"Can I help?" a deep bass voice purred.

"Dammit, that hurt! Oh, excuse me, but that did

hurt" was her reaction to being startled to the point of bumping her head on the trunk cover.

"I'm sorry for surprising you. I truly am. That was not the impression I intended. I'm Lane Hamilton, and you have to be Cass that I have heard so much about." His grin and twinkling eyes accented his sincerity.

"In turn, I hadn't intended to appear like an ostrich, either. But, hi, anyway." Rubbing the bump on her head while handing him the bag of toys, Cass slammed the trunk lid. She was impressed with his attire, a soft chamois shirt with a deep vee at the throat and snug-fitting jeans, so very masculine, like a tall, broad-shouldered athlete. *Cut those thoughts right now,* she thought to herself. But she couldn't help expelling her breath in a long, wistful sigh.

The aroma of dinner wafted throughout the house. Amy, also in jeans, approached the coffee table with a tray of sparkling burgundy in a cut-glass decanter and matching wine glasses.

"Chad and I are so happy to have company, as obviously, Nell and Millie are. Dinner is not quite ready, so let's put our feet up for awhile."

"It smells luscious, Amy. This is a real treat for me, a home-cooked meal and relaxing company." Lane chose to place his wine and elbow on the mantle, totally at ease. An aura of calm authority seemed to surround him.

Watch yourself! Cass thought. *But he does have a face that seems boyish, a square and strong jawline with a curious little dent in the center of it—astonishingly handsome and virile, clean shaven with a rugged, thoroughly male sort of beauty. His smile is devastating—a forceful and vital man. His ability to put everyone at ease is enviable!*

14

Aloud she reprimanded herself. "Stop it, Cass! Your libido is running away with you. If he looks as good in his bathing suit as he does relaxing at the mantle, you are in deep trouble again. Don't even think about it! Perish those troublesome thoughts *right now!* Promise that you will never find yourself alone with Lane. You have suffered enough and you *do not need him!"*

It was time to deal out their toys—water pistols, three minis and one power gun, with Chad getting the power gun. Everybody had changed into their bathing suits, and Chad's eyes sparkled with an impish grin.

"Are we choosing teams, or are we on our own?"

"We're on our own, but no hiding behind anything. All action is out in the open. It's distance and tactics that count. We each start from our own corner of the yard to plan strategy."

With lots of shrieking, barking, and thorough soaking, the game lasted until the huge tub of water was entirely depleted—only three time-outs for refills. Chad loved it, which was the name of the game. Showers and dry clothes were definitely in order, and Cass and Amy could have made good use of a hair dresser, but it really wasn't necessary. They both were blessed with natural curls that fell easily into place, thankfully, as they both professed.

After toweling down Millie and Nell and drying Chad's wheelchair and braces, they all retired to the lounge chairs to discuss the winner. Chad was obviously beginning to tire, and the sun was descending behind the wooded copse of pines.

"Dear ladies, you have challenged us men to the end of our rope, so it's time for me to crawl back to my quarters. Thank you for the great home cooking and showing me how to have fun again." Amy, Cass, and Chad promptly agreed to call it a day as soon as Lane left the yard.

"Can we do something like this again soon, Cass? Wait'll the kids at school hear about it, and maybe we can have some of them come over to compete if they have their own weapons."

"Of course we will if Amy allows such ruffians in action again," and she winked at Amy. "Now it's time for me to go home and regroup for whatever comes next. Thanks so much for the gourmet dinner, Amy, and for sharing your friends. Please call me soon."

Taking the long route home gave Cass the much needed time to think. She knew that her thoughts were taking her right onto the skeet-shooting range again. To herself aloud, "Be aware, gal! Keep focused! Your only involvement there is dear little crippled Chad, *not* Lane Hamilton!" But all manner of chemistry was in action, and somehow she knew that it was reciprocal. She couldn't afford even an approach to recognizing the tingling throughout her entire body when near Lane. It was up to her to break this threatening pattern *right now.*

She was tired but needed company. Luckily Sue was at home, and as she came rushing out to Cass's car, bubbling with news of her latest golf score, she realized that Cass was not receptive to her mood. In fact, Cass appeared glum!

"How did Amy's dinner party go? Is Lane really a hunk?" Cass just smiled, nodded in the affirmative and stated simply that she didn't want to discuss that subject.

"Oh, oh, a personality clash?"

"Nope, just need some time to survey the situation, although I have agreed to tutor Chad while he is hospitalized and during recovery. He is such a sweetheart, and I'm astounded at the bonding that has taken place between us. Getting him back to normal is my prime project right now. He and Amy are so fortunate to have each other, as they have both filled a massive void, having lost Chad's dad, Todd, so abruptly. She is totally involved in Chad's recovery, too. It appears now that he may be out of that damnable wheelchair and free of his braces in seven to eight months. Daily, I pray for that."

"Then what, Cass? Can Amy handle his future alone? She's a busy gal, but probably can do it as her office is in her home. Is there any chemistry between Amy and Lane? That would be the ideal situation wouldn't it."

Cass's heart dropped right down to the soles of her feet. That thought had never occurred to her. If that were the case, the whole scenario would be a convoluted disaster. But she vowed that she would battle any odds until Chad's complete recovery.

"At this point, Sue, we can take it only a day at a time. Eventually, I do want to go back to Alaska and take Chad with me. We have already discussed it, which makes him all the more determined to become whole and strong again. Plans like that will help him to fight the pain and boredom during the weeks of treatments and therapy that he faces. Gotta scurry now. I'm right next to being a litter case from exhaustion."

During the drive home, Lane's boyish grin appeared on her windshield, and his strong, broad-shouldered torso rode in the seat beside her, showing his angular jawline and the sensuous curve of his lips. Every bright red car was a Corvette with Massachusetts license plates. She muttered to herself, "Good God, what kind of escapism do I need to avoid this obsession? I don't even know the guy. Am I cracking? For damned sure this is one problem that I can't divulge to Amy."

Thankfully the peace and serenity of her home soothed Cass's nerves. "Have a drink, watch the news, and hopefully, things will appear differently tomorrow. Of course they will. I'm the one who has control of what I think, *so just don't think about him!* Right!" Finally she slipped into her favorite powder-blue satin nightie and totally collapsed. "I wonder if blue is Lane's favorite color. Maybe he'd like red satin sheets instead of blue. Oh, God, here I go again!" Finally curled into a tight fetal position, she slept, only to dream.

His body was perfection, causing her whole being to tremble. His hands caressed her breasts, while his tongue feathered her turgid nipples—pure ecstasy! How could her body betray her, responding to the advances of someone she had just met. Her legs parted for his insistent probing toward her private woman's place. God, his mouth could do all that? "Take me now, Lane!" He entered her with ease but withheld his orgasm until they both exploded. His moans coming from the pillow smothered in her damp hair woke her with her own breathless panting.

She bolted upright instantly and glanced at the clock. Damn her dreaming! It was four o'clock in the morning, and she was desolately alone. "Get up, have some cocoa, and stop trembling. After all, it was only a dream. Try to remember the promise you made to yourself about keeping separate from anything that can cause anguish, and this has all the possibilities of just that."

15

Lane had fared no better on his way home from Amy's dinner. He pensively retraced the occasion from the minute he had met Cass in the driveway to her mysterious smile when he left. The woman had made an impression on him that was not among his past experiences. He did not believe in the hogwash of clicking body chemistry, but what else was it that he had experienced? Good God, his hormones were in complete chaos! His racing thoughts were *Back off, kid, you know nothing about this gal. She is attractive, wholesome, compassionate, and does have a fun-loving sense of humor.* She had made no attempt to impress him as a sex kitten, but it happened. *Hell, her blue bathing suit had been almost prudish, but dammit, her body wasn't. Better get off that line of thought, my friend. We will be crossing paths frequently at the hospital, so let's try to keep the association impersonal, strictly platonic. Now that's the order of things if only my hormones can be convinced of my intent.*

His driveway was a welcome sight. Lane wasn't certain whether he was physically or emotionally exhausted, probably a combination of both. The answering machine showed a number of calls, but the one he had hoped for took precedence over all. The results of Chad's screening clinic had been completed, and he was to be admitted into the Springfield unit of the Shriners Hospital for Crippled Children as soon as possible. Lane was ecstatic and immediately called Amy. They agreed to transfer Chad's school records, and both he and Amy would admit Chad the following Monday morning. Should he call Cass? No, don't push it. Have Amy call her with the good news. After all, her tutoring wouldn't begin until Chad was settled in and accustomed to his schedule. To hell with it! Call her. It might be weeks before he had reason to contact her again.

"Hello," came the gentle, purring, voice. Lane was as breathless as a schoolboy waiting for Cass to answer the phone.

"Hi, Cass, just had to share some good news. Chad will be admitted next Monday morning."

Cass could barely speak. She had expected to hear anyone's voice but Lane's. Somehow in the back of her mind, she recognized that he didn't even have to announce who he was. Had his voice haunted her to the extent that it was not necessary? Did he think that?

"How wonderful, Lane. I had no idea that it would be so soon. Chad and Amy must be even more deliriously happy to hear that than I am, if that's possible. Thanks so much for calling, and I certainly will make myself available for any assistance that I can offer until his tutoring can begin. Do keep me posted."

"I'll do that, Cass. I'm sure that Chad is trying to get your line to share his good news, so I'll keep this brief. Tomorrow morning I shall go to Springfield to make very certain that all is in order, so take care, and hopefully, I will see you soon."

"'Bye, Lane, and thanks so much for calling."

Cass's mind scrambled. Had she been too abrupt? Had he expected numerous questions when none were forthcoming? Perhaps that was her appeal. She seemed not to get involved in idle chatter. Maybe he had been too abrupt. I'd better not get into any more speculation. Get some rest. Tomorrow will be a busy day.

A long, relaxing shower, one scotch, and the caress of his silk, red polka-dot pajamas put Lane to sleep almost immediately. Hopefully, his dreams would be pleasant ones. They were. Cass's beautiful naked body was totally responsive, no silly childlike inhibitions for her. She had known adult love and had the same pounding need for affection as he. They were not strangers in his bed as he kissed her gently and she responded aggressively. Her nails made the muscles of his back ripple and his manhood rapidly respond. The first orgasm was spontaneously shared, and almost immediately, he was brought to peak again. They both soared off into the cosmos together and returned together, again massively erupting with breathless gasps. His own moans awoke him. Dammit, his bed was empty!

Lane's digital clock read five A.M. At least he had had some sleep. How totally fulfilling it would be to stay in bed and go on with that dream. But he was due at the hospital early, so a prolonged cold shower, scalding hot coffee, and catching the early morning news while driving his Vette should put him back on track. He must have everything cleared at the hospital before Amy and Chad arrived.

Fantasies of Cass wove in and out of his thoughts. When would he see her again? How would he react? Control, mister, don't scare her off. I can call her tonight when Chad's schedule is firmly in place. Don't play games with her. She will run. After all, the part she would be playing in Chad's success was far more important than his embryonic plans right now. Plans? What plans did he really have in mind? God, but he *was* sick of living alone. Cass would be such a sincere and fun companion. What a helluva word, companion. He wanted far more than a companion. Perhaps he should check her out thoroughly before making any commitment even to himself. Dare he trust his instincts only? He must not discuss any of his feelings with Amy, as it might throw a wrench into the close relationship of them all working together for Chad's sake. Focus on Chad, dummy.

But if yesterday was any preview of what time spent with Cass meant, it would be difficult to avoid any more personal contact in the very near future. I can call her re Chad's progress, but can I be elsewhere when it is time for her to start tutoring? Don't speculate. Play it one day at a time, and see what happens. But any more dreams like last night certainly wouldn't help his plans to follow a cooling-off period. He'd just have to keep reminding himself to downshift and coast for a while.

16

Dr. Amy had very little time to reflect on her plans after receiving Lane's phone call. She and Chad had talked to Cass, packed what they thought necessary for the time being, and retired early. She certainly would sleep peacefully, as her problems did not manifest themselves in dreams. Hers were real.

Dr. Amy Fielding had not escaped the emotional turmoil of Chad's problems. It brought back memories of her failed marriage to Chad's autocratic, manipulating grandfather, Arnold. His death had left her with a minor degree of sorrow, almost apathy, but the death of his son, Todd, was bruisingly traumatic. Even though she hadn't been close to Todd and Jill recently, she had been a major part of Todd's life in his early years.

The time was fast approaching when she must share with Cass her investigative results about Archer. Was Cass ready to face this yet? Should she wait for Chad's full or maybe even partial recovery? Cass's deep involvement with Chad seemed to be keeping her on an even keel presently. Should she interrupt a gratifying episode in Cass's life just yet? Should she discuss the damnable problem with Lane? His advice might help, but shouldn't she wait until Lane knew Cass a bit better? But what did Lane have to do with it?

Holy Toledo! Her mind was racing out of control. Put it on the back burner for now, kid. Lock all the pain involved behind a mask, cut your losses and aggravations, try for a good night's sleep, and get on with it. You have a big day tomorrow, and after all, you do have other patients, too. What if something happened to me, and Cass never knew the truth about Archer!? At least put it all in writing and leave it in a sealed envelope with Lane in case of my demise. That's it. That's what I'll do for now. At least Cass would be with someone supportive when the shock of its contents was revealed. I'll do just that when I get back from Springfield.

The most valuable contribution I can make is to Chad right now. He needs my strength. I wonder how long he will be confined. Perhaps he can go to France with me when I follow up on my research work that I've looked forward to for years. But then I would have to wait until Cass brought him back from that Alaskan tour, which he is counting on. Okay, that's settled. Relax with a cup of tea and get some sleep, as it's going to be a long drive tomorrow and I must get Chad ready to leave early. As the house seemed to settle with a sigh into peaceful quietude, Amy slept.

Chad, as well, had not entirely escaped the preentry hospital jitters. But as most youngsters of his age, the thoughts that scampered about were for the most part positive. Could the Shriners Hospital doctors really turn him from a cripple to a normal, strong-legged guy once again? Would he truly escape his wheelchair and braces? Would he and Cass really go to Alaska? He wished that his dad and mom could be here, but did not allow himself to flounder around in self-pity. He knew the reality that Dad and Mom were gone forever, but he kept them in his prayers every night. He somehow knew that they were with him in spirit. He thought about how lucky he was not to be entirely alone. After all, he had Granny Amy, and Granny Cass, and Lane. How many orphaned kids had people like them on their team? He chuckled as he dropped off to sleep thinking that he'd better not call them granny! Amy and Cass seemed too young for that, and any grannies that he had ever heard about did *not* participate in water-pistol battles. Chad drifted into pleasant dreams of walking on the Mendenhall glacier, playing with malemute puppies and baby seals and real Eskimo kids in an igloo.

Five o'clock came early, but they were ready. Having packed the night before, they hugged Nell and Millie, promising to return as soon as possible. If Amy spent the night in Springfield, Cass would be over to keep them company. The day promised to be crisp and sparkling, and Amy figured on about a two-and-a-half-hour drive with at least one stop at a McDonald's somewhere, a treat that Chad always looked forward to.

"S'pose Lane will be there to meet us? Is the hospital in the city or the country? I wonder how many other kids there are there! Would they allow him to keep Dirigo, his good-luck, tiny black bear, with him? Dirigo had even survived the plane crash, so he must be lucky. Dirigo was a Maine black bear; his name was the motto of the State of Maine." Chad hugged Dirigo tighter and secretly promised that they would not be separated if at all possible.

Amy answered only the very direct questions, thankful that Chad was in such good spirits. He was certainly facing this experience with the stamina of a person of a more advanced age. God knows that if she were headed into this, she would be a basket case before it even happened. But Chad had already survived a tough trauma, which had obviously given him strength to face the future. She must put her major decisions on hold until this situation stabilized, when she could think and plan more rationally.

Dr. Lane Hamilton had kept his vigil near the hospital entrance and was on the front steps when Amy's ranch wagon arrived. With an encouraging grin, he was waving another black bear.

"Hi, you two. I'm glad Dirigo came, too, 'cause this fella, Alaska, needs a friend!"

Chad was ecstatic. That answered his two biggest questions. Lane was here and Dirigo could stay. Wow, this was going to be a piece of cake. He'd enter in a wheelchair, but he vowed that he would walk out.

17

The past months had developed into a deep relationship between Cass and Lane, far beyond the expectations of either. Just previous to the Thanksgiving holiday, Lane had planned a festive gathering for all concerned. Chad could not leave the hospital, but Amy, Cass, and he would spend most of the day with Chad, then retire to the apartment for drinks and dinner with their friends on the hospital staff.

Chad had become everyone's hope and promise, so the conversation bubbled around his recovery. Lane knew that Amy would have to return home to Nell and Millie, but there was little need for Cass to leave, as he saw it. She could return to her quarters early in the morning if he could convince her to stay. After all, the whole staff knew that they had become very close during the past weeks of Chad's therapy.

Amy left fairly early, and the other guests filtered away miserably slowly in Lane's mind. He wanted to be alone with Cass, and he sensed that she was not looking forward to spending another lonely night in her quarters.

Cass had eaten lightly, resulting in her favorite champagne quietly sneaking in its relaxing results. She stalled while stacking the dishwasher and generally tidied the apartment while continuing with intermittent idle chatter. She reminded herself that her mind had been made up never to give away her heart again, and she had not been in the slightest danger of doing so. She had enjoyed the camaraderie of other men but had not felt even a spark of attraction—until Lane, who had triggered something long-buried inside her. There was something about him that drew her like a moth, closer and closer to a flame. Could she stay away from him? No man could duplicate that rare combination of carefully cultivated sophistication and rare animal magnetism.

Wholly conscious of his close proximity, all her senses were screamingly aware of him. He smelled of soap and tobacco, radiating a disturbing warmth... so tall and handsome, so virile. She must avoid his touch, as she knew that that would be devastating. She must be cautious. Her kind of grief and trauma had been like a deep mountain fissure that she had climbed from, hand over hand. Would she have the stamina to go through that again? And although something within her mind censored her actions, something stronger claimed that little mattered except this man beside her. Another sip brought forth a why not have a what-the-hell day. If it's going to be, it's gotta be me.

As Cass approached Lane with one more fluted glass of champagne, his eyebrows shot up questioningly. Was she melting? With interlocked elbows, their bodies meshed. The impact of his first kiss was profound. She wanted to melt into the ground and disappear. Then she felt that she could soar over the clouds and fly forever. His kiss was wickedly dangerous, bringing from her throat a soft moan of delight. Still throbbingly embraced, Lane ever so slowly backed her toward the bedroom and his massive king-sized bed.

Shuddering ripples of desire shook her entire being as they recklessly tossed each article of clothing into space, letting it land wherever. With teasing enticement, his head bent, his mouth tracing the paths his hands had taken as she instinctively arched toward him. Boldly, she fenced with his tongue as he explored with hot, steamy kisses. He trembled at her response. Her body became a throbbing volcanic storm, aching for something beyond her reach and understanding. A fire coiled like a serpent in the pit of her stomach, stealing throughout her body in hot fluid rushes that left her weakly whimpering. The hot, hard ache within her had to ease.

His solid heat pressing against her finally entered her throbbing vagina as she matched his rhythm with fevered anticipation. The soaring emotion and fiery pulsing of her heated blood flowed like lava through her veins. Release came in a blinding flash of contracting muscles and pulsing flesh washing over her in drowning waves. His tongue and mouth plundered the very core of her existence, draining her totally, then once again raising her to the very highest pinnacle of pleasure's peak. Joined in rapture with a rhythmic binding, they spiraled upward on waves of sensual bliss, which crashed around them in the delight of passion's fulfillment.

When breathless and spent, and her heart pounding so fiercely that she could feel her entire body vibrate, Cass sleepily smiled, cuddled closer, and promptly drifted into a deep sleep. Lane drew her closer and slept soundly.

18

A soft purring awoke Cass.

"What in the world is that? Where am I? Oh, no, not still in Lane's bed, and he's not here. That's his alarm. Shut the damn thing off. What time is it? Where *is* Lane? Dammit, I've been conned again!" She tiptoed to the bathroom listening and hoping that Lane might be in the kitchen. "Probably not, you sucker! How will I ever be able to face him at the hospital again? I must go. There's no way that I can disappoint Chad. Hell, it's nine o'clock, and everyone will know. Okay, dumb ass, face it. Face it. You started it, and now try to get yourself out of this one."

In haste, Cass dressed, grabbed her purse with the car keys, and raced for the door. She still had to go to her own quarters to shower and change. "The damned phone is ringing. To hell with it, let it ring!" Her mind was in complete chaos. "Shall I stop for coffee? No! Move it! You are probably right back where you started—a clay pigeon—again! Does he know something about my background? Had their friendship been a subterfuge leading up to a one-night stand? Had it all been just fun and games in Lane's mind? But he had seemed so sincere. So have others, dummy. There is no way to avoid facing him this morning, but I cannot and will not let Chad down. Just brave it through by acting nonchalantly? Kiddo, that won't be easy after last night. Why didn't he wake me? Couldn't face his own conscience probably, just split. But all this doesn't fit what I thought I knew about his character. We'll see. Just bury it for now, and get back to the hospital. Shall I go to my quarters first and change? Of course, idiot, you haven't even showered yet.

"Here goes nothing, kid, get cracking. Hm-m, he did leave the coffee pot turned on. Well, turn it off and travel. Whatever will happen will happen." It was then she spied the note taped to the front door knob. "Oh, oh, probably a Dear Joan note. Why am I trembling?"

In Lane's inimitable block print, it read, "Hopefully we can have dinner tonight, Sleeping Beauty."

"Do I really want to do that? I have to face him sometime, but I absolutely must have time to think, or in the teenage vernacular, I need space. Somehow I'll think of something before we cross paths this morning. For now, just concentrate on Chad's welfare."

Cass spent very little time showering and dressing, intermittently sipping ice-cold orange juice and hot, steaming coffee. Her sports car purred toward the hospital with a soothing sonata from her concert sound stereo doing little to settle her jangled nerves. "Thankfully, it isn't a gray day. The sparkling sun does help, and my canary-yellow cashmere helps lift me partially out of this gug. It's Chad's favorite, too, and I must not let any depression surface in his presence, as he has enough to contend with right now. He may be already upset that I am running late or may even be thinking that I won't show at all. Suppose Lane has been to see him this morning?"

Chad had been transferred to a wheelchair for the first time since his latest surgery. "Hi, Sleeping Beauty, I hoped that you wouldn't miss my Thanksgiving surprise for you. They'll only allow me in my wheels until lunch, but it feels great to move around, Cass. And you even wore my favorite dress for a celebration that you didn't even suspect."

Through tears of gratitude, Cass gave Chad her standard bear hug.

"I'm so proud of you, Chad, and please forgive me for being late. Seeing you like this gives us all so much to be thankful for, and thanks for the new nickname. How did you know that I overslept?"

"Oh, Lane was here very early and told me about his dinner party and that it had gone on quite a long time and that you hadn't gone home until late, late, late, so you were probably pretty tired. He's the one who said we'd tease you with 'Sleeping Beauty'! He won't be back until late today, because he was called to the Shriners Burns Institute in Boston. Gosh, he's a great guy, and I'm wicked lucky. I know that he had a long drive, but he still took time to come to see me before he left. He wanted to be here for the surprise, too, but as he said, 'Duty calls.' I s'pose now that I can sit up, my homework is going to get heavier, huh? Okay, I'm ready. It is going to be easier to write out my assignments sitting up, too."

"Not necessarily true, but that's possible, Tiger."

"I wonder if Amy is coming today. Maybe not though, 'cause she had to drive all the way home last night. S'pose she can ever bring Nell and Millie here? I sure do miss 'em, don't you?"

19

Dr. Amy Fielding didn't visit Chad that day. While checking her mail early that morning, she received more shocking news. A full report had come in on Archer, leaving her with volcanic emotions. Her thoughts scampered aimlessly with startling questions. *Had I known or even suspected all this, would I have pursued the present path? Would I have taken Cass as a client at all? What direction should I take from here? This is going to be a tough one for all involved. Considering the present circumstances, wouldn't it be more expedient to file all of this material until a later date? That will give me a longer cooling-off period and a chance to plot a more opportune moment to share the shock.* Wouldn't right now be the time to put into effect her dream of attending The Sorbonne? That would not only give her time but also space, and Paris could be just what she needed. It wouldn't come as a surprise to anyone; hadn't she discussed her dream plan with everyone in her circle, including Lane, Chad, and Cass? At that time, the whole idea had been a more or less embryonic fantasy. But was there any earthly reason that she could not follow through and make it a reality? *Do it!*

Number one on the list of "things to do" was to call the Sorbonne for details on registration, scheduling, and living quarters. Number two, as soon as the date was confirmed, to notify all clients of her plans and arrange for her replacement in their schedules. Number three was to plot her flight plans, and number four, invite Cass and Chad to stay in her home with Nell and Millie.

Would they accept? Hopefully. That would solve so many problems and put her mind totally at easy in that category. After all, Lane, Cass, and Chad had discussed a trip to Alaska in a motor home and had already asked whether they could take Millie and Nell with them. It just might work. Seal Archer's report away for now, and erase it from her mind. She knew that Cass would be asking about her investigation, but somehow she would stall and hope that all of Cass's planned activities would soothe her anxieties, at least for the time being. Amy was certain that the right time to reveal the information would present itself. Lock it away. This is no time to be indecisive. Start the ball rolling right now.

Amy checked her files for the telephone connection to the Sorbonne. The registrars were already aware of her qualifications for advanced research, so matters of admission should be solved fairly readily. And they were. Even she was stunned with the results of the initial contact. They would Fax all relevant material promptly. Within the month, she could choose her dates of attendance, giving her time to arrange all affairs at home. Great!

The next step was to discuss her itinerary with Lane and Cass. Okay, plan a simple luncheon right here and soon. There was no need to include Chad in these ideas at present. Why get him involved until plans were more definite. Now for protocol; should she share all this with Lane first for his reaction? Was Cass in more of a position to help make the decisions? No! Three heads are better than two to sift through all the what-ifs.

Cass was in her quarters at eight that evening when the phone rang.

"Hi, Cass, it's Amy. It seems like eons since I've seen you, but my schedule has been nothing less than chaotic. I do have some ideas that I'd like to discuss with you and Lane, just the three of us. Can you find some time when both of you can get away for lunch or dinner here at the house? It is tremendously important to me, and I really do need your help in making some decisions. No, dear, it has nothing to do with Archer. It is mostly about your plans to take Chad to Alaska, okay? I'll work around whatever schedule that you two have available."

"Sounds great, Amy, no problems I hope, but if there are, we are always there for you, you know that. I'll speak to Lane tomorrow morning at the hospital and call you right away."

"No, it's nothing earth-shattering. I think you both will have a positive reaction to most of it anyway. I'll be looking forward to hearing from you. I've missed you, and Millie and Nell do, too. I wouldn't mention this to Chad presently. He would feel hurt to be left out of a home visit, right?"

20

Chad had suffered far more than anyone realized, but he had not complained, ever. He knew how fortunate he was to have so many people pulling for him, and he didn't want to worry them. The plane crash had interrupted their lives as well as his, and he would not ignore that fact. They had their own lives to live, their own dreams and hopes. He promised himself that he would work very hard toward full recovery, which would be one of the successes in their lives and hopefully repay them in some degree for all their time and energy. And the therapist had convinced him that a positive outlook to the future was a big part of his gaining strength toward being a whole person again. He also knew that not many of the other crippled children at this hospital had the fun things to look forward to that he did, so he must be careful not to talk too much about his trip to Alaska. How many of them had been promised anything like that as soon as they were completely knit and free from pain. He must try to help others to make complete recovery their main goal in life, too.

He could not upset Lane, Cass, and Amy about his tortuous nightmares about the accident. The realistic dreams, that high whistle of descent as the plane took its fatal downward path to earth, of the rasping screech of twisting metal when the plane's wings were torn away as they hit the trees, of the shrieks of pain that had been stamped into his consciousness before he passed into oblivion. The last thought that had flashed through Chad's mind was that his dad had called the 747 the best aircraft ever made, a big pussycat.

It couldn't be happening! His therapist had promised that those memories would fade with time, but he had his doubts. More often now, his mom and dad were appearing at the foot of his bed. They were always together and smiling, both showing the thumbs-up signal, sending him the message that they, too, were there for him. His therapist said that those were their spirits and that they were now like his guardian angels. He had told Lane about that and wished that Lane could see them, too. After all, he had been their friend before they had solved life's greatest mystery.

Chad was extremely relieved and proud that Lane had removed the calliper from his right leg, but the left, where the muscles had suffered severe damage, was weaker and still needed the support of the steel frame. Daily, he was exercising with weights, knowing that he would eventually walk with a slight limp and one day that, too, would disappear.

He thought a lot about that trip to Alaska and wished that he could talk about it to the other kids, but he was too sensitive and knew that it would only make them feel bad. He didn't mention it to Lane, Cass, or Amy either, just in case something prohibited their plans. He knew that they were entirely serious, but did not want to badger them about how and when. They had mentioned renting a motor home. Wow, would that ever be an experience, especially with Nell and Millie traveling with them! That way he wouldn't have to fly, but he was certain that he would overcome that fear, too. He must never let them know of his reluctance to ever board another plane. What if that became an option? He would have to handle it when the time came.

Christmas music was now wafting from all the radio

and television stations. The hospital was not Chad's choice of places to stay during the holidays, but having no choice, he would try to enter into the spirit. He wished that he could buy gifts for Lane, Cass, and Amy, the doctors, nurses, and especially all the other kids, but the best he could do right now was to be cheerful and help boost the morale of others. The sure thing that he could accomplish was to make them all laugh at his off-key singing when they sang Christmas carols together. He knew that he was amusing, so he tried to sing louder than the rest and act as though he didn't realize the reason for their fun. Meanwhile he could make his own Christmas cards in the activity room.

Lane and Cass said that they would be away for a day or two, and he wondered why. It seemed strange that they hadn't given a reason, and it was even stranger that Amy hadn't visited for so long. But he didn't forget that he had been promised a big surprise when they returned. His hospital room window faced the front of the building and was where he spent many hours waiting for that sleek, red Corvette or the silver Buick to come gliding in. Down deep, his hope was that the "big surprise" wasn't a visit from Santa Claus. He was too mature for that, but they didn't have kids, so they might think that it would be a big deal. In that case, he would play their game, but he really had to do so anyway because some of the other kids were still believers.

On the third day, as Chad was rubbing the sleep from his eyes, he rolled over to watch the driveway from the big, sunny picture window beside his bed. He was becoming anxious, but worrying wouldn't bring them back any sooner. At least someone was having company or it might be a new patient. Boy, whoever it was sure traveled in style—a massive Pace Arrow motor home. Wow, if only Lane were here to see it! But there was no time to be thinking about anything else, as he was already running late. He must get to his lengthy and strenuous physical therapy session.

21

Dressed and ready for his appointment, Chad stood at the window, enjoying a last few minutes lovingly studying that fantastic motor home—real cool wheels. He was late already and figured a few more minutes wouldn't hurt. Behind him, the door quietly and slowly opened.

"Hi, Tiger, we finally made it! And guess what, no therapy session today. We finagled a day off for you, so let's go out to breakfast." Chad was so shakingly excited that he bypassed his crutches and while hanging onto the edge of the bed struggled into Cass's arms.

"Gosh, I've missed you. Where's Amy? Can I take Alaska and Dirigo with me? They haven't been off the grounds for a long time either, or are we going to the cafeteria, Lane?"

"No, my good buddy, no cafeteria. We're going to hit the road for the day. I'll carry our black bear mascots while you get your jacket and maneuver those crutches. Let's escape," grinned Lane.

"Could I just show you something before we leave? Please just look out my window at what drove up while I was looking for you. Isn't that a beauty, Lane? Could you drive something as big as that? Doesn't your Vette look like a toy beside it?"

"I have all the faith in the world that Lane can do anything. C'mon we're outa' here!" Cass chortled, fighting back tears.

Hurrying down the corridor behind Lane and Cass, Chad wondered why they were headed for the front door rather than the parking lot at the rear of the hospital, where Cass kept her car. There was no way that three people could ride in the Vette, but they must be going to try it. That would really be a treat. When they approached the red Corvette, Cass opened the driver's door.

"Ten more steps and you are entering your *big surprise,*" Lane announced.

"Holy Toledo, is this for real? I can't believe it's true, or am I dreaming? Are we going in it now?"

Lane opened the door, and there, nose to nose with Chad were Nell and Millie doubling from neck to tail with their joy at seeing Chad for the first time in many, many days.

"Back up you two, and let Chad get in!" Chad's eyes slowly followed up to the top step, and there crouched Amy, trying to pull the dogs away from the door.

"Hi, and welcome to The Chariot. You thought I'd never get here, didn't you? And I need a hug as soon as I get untangled from your buddies."

Chad was totally overwhelmed with so much happening all at once. With tears about to flow, he turned to Lane with sheer worship in his eyes.

"It's really yours? We're honest to gosh going for a ride in it? Gee, Amy, I've missed you. Where's Cass?"

"Not only are we going for a ride, but we're going to have breakfast aboard. How's that for breaking up the monotony? Cass has taken my car around to the parking lot, and we'll pick her up there, okay? Let's get settled in for our shakedown cruise."

Beside the driver were front seats that made up into a double chaise longue.

"That's your spot, Chad. You, Nell, and Millie are riding shotgun. Do you think this can make it to Alaska and back? Let's pick up Cass, and I'll give you the grand tour when we stop for breakfast."

Chad stashed his crutches and climbed onto the assigned spot, his eyes trying to take in everything at once while fumbling to fasten his seat belt. The engine purred to life as they slowly glided to the parking lot to meet Cass. She boarded with another big hug for Chad.

"Thanks for remembering to pick up the cook, guys." Her eyes were sparkling with thoughts that she had never been happier.

Their destination was an expansive rest area near the Quabbin Reservoir. Chad was ecstatic. Comments and questions flowed and, in his excitement, never waited for answers.

"Jeepers, we're up so high, we're looking right down on the other traffic. It's so long, Lane, how can you get it around sharp corners? Have you practiced? Is this what is really called a shakedown cruise? I can't believe that we can eat and cook and play games and sleep at the same time that we're moving. Where do we all sleep? You're going to Alaska with us aren't you, Amy? When are we really going?"

"Whoa, slow down, Tiger. Let's enjoy today first, and then we'll discuss our trip. It's looking now as though we just might be on the road close to Christmas. How does that sound? Just a short time more, and we will be history in Springfield."

At the rest stop, Chad's curiosity was still flaming as he checked out the stove, oven, refrigerator, and bathroom.

"Wow, even a shower and two TVs, one in the dinette and one in the bedroom. Where do I sleep? Gee, even bedspreads. Aren't we going to use sleeping bags? And look at all the places to store stuff. It's built just like a submarine, Lane. Every nook and cranny has a built-in something. What's that crank for, a built-in antenna? And air conditioning, too? Man, some kinda' luxury, huh? I can hardly wait to get started. Can you drive it, too, Cass?"

While Amy and Cass prepared brunch and set the

dinette table for four, Lane and Chad took the dogs for a walk. It was difficult to tear Chad away from the RV, as he wanted to know all about the storage units, hoses, generator, and utility hook-ups. He realized that he couldn't climb the rear ladder to the sun deck on top right now, but that would be a goal for the future.

During brunch, Amy explained that they were taking her and the dogs back home for now. She expounded on her plans to go to France while they were in Alaska, and yes, Millie and Nell would be traveling with them. There was lots to do in preparation. Each one could make out a list of what should be packed; then when they combined the lists, they could cross out luxury items if necessary.

"Isn't that a great project to work on until departure time? I will take care of the papers, health certificates, etcetera that you will need for Nell and Millie. I'm sure that I'll see you a number of times before we go our separate ways, and then we can swap addresses and telephone numbers to keep in touch. It's beginning to look like the greatest Christmas that any of us had even suspected, right?"

Hopefully, that would be true, but why did a dark ominous cloud of apprehension seem to descend upon Lane?

22

The damn "downer" feeling still held. Couldn't it be a triple low in my biorhythms that Cass so firmly believed in, or could it? While Lane's thoughts ran wildly rampant, Cass and Chad were exploring the motor home more thoroughly. He heard sleeping arrangements being discussed but secretly vowed that those plans would change in his favor. That was one more hurdle to master, and the sooner the better.

He could not erase the picture of Amy's face when they left her driveway today. Her demeanor appeared to Lane to be one of fighting to control her emotions. Why were her expressive eyes shining with tears ready to spill? Millie and Nell were loyally standing on each side of Amy, her white-knuckled hands grasping their collars. Why were their tails dejectedly hanging between their legs? They must already be missing Chad, of course. But why should Amy be experiencing any negative emotions?

To expand his agitation, huge snowflakes began to splash on the massive windshield. Hell, he didn't recall any storm being forecast, but the western sky was turning an ominous dark gray, and they were headed straight into it. Actually, that was no problem presently, as they were fast approaching the hospital. If there was a weather problem, he could leave the RV in the hospital parking lot. The approaching storm with no warning pushed his mind into questioning the wisdom of heading to Alaska in the dead of winter, when the weather could be strangely unpredictable. Wouldn't a trip to Disneyland and a tour of the southern coast make more sense during this season? Could Cass and Chad be convinced of that?

Everything was moving much too fast for Lane's orderly mind. Due to the exuberance at Chad's fast recovery, keeping in mind that he had not yet gained back full strength, he and Cass were overlooking some must-be-dones before departing into cold climes for an extended period. Wouldn't the warm beaches be much more favorable for Chad's exercise regime? Possibly he could get someone on the hospital staff to suggest this. And wouldn't it be safer to have an extended shakedown cruise in warm weather? And just possibly, Chad's best friend, Tommy, could join them. So many things to do, now that reality had set in. But presently, the project was to get them all safely back to Springfield, settle Chad into his room, go back to his apartment with Cass, and discuss the problems one at a time.

Leaving Chad at the hospital was not as traumatic as Lane had expected. Chad was so exhausted that he collapsed on his bed while reminding Lane of the promise that he would park the motor home where Chad could see it from his room. When they were parked and ready to leave the grounds, they looked up to see Chad at his window giving them a final wave good-bye. Strange little lad, couldn't rest, probably for fear of losing someone else.

Lane was thankful that Cass was one who loved the Van Cliburn tapes of his concert-sound stereo in the Corvette. That gave him time to think on his way back to his quarters. But he decided that because it was getting near the dinner hour, they should eat out. They both loved Paoli's Parlor, typically dark and Italian, with red-checkered table cloths and dripping candles in Chianti bottles, where they could sip Barolo out of thick greenish glasses. And besides, he had been waiting for this chance for some time, and right now he needed this type of ambiance for what he had to say to Cass.

Lane had known for some time that Cass was the one

with whom he wanted to spend the rest of his life. He knew of her past and her tireless search for Archer. He wanted to be part of her life, to help and protect her if she would have him. Cass was a proudly independent lady, who had been deeply hurt and was still licking her wounds but seemed to have finally managed to stem the flow of blood. She would be difficult to convince, but now was the time to cast all trepidation asunder and make an attempt to solve his biggest problem. Thankfully, he had prepared for this in advance and silently prayed that it would not be an exercise in futility.

23

Cass was certainly not insensitive to Lane's mood. He seemed to be battling a private problem, or was it personal? Dare she think that she could attempt to invade his thought processes? She did love him so much and could not bear to see him upset to any degree. Questions were blowing through her mind like leaves in the wind, never snagging themselves on an answer. Hopefully, Lane would share his reasons for such a somber mood during dinner. Right now, he needed to concentrate on driving through some treacherous territory.

Paoli was serving them their dinner personally, so pleased with the company of Dr. Lane and Cassio, as he called her. They had been there so many times in the past that Paoli loved them as part of his family. He always remembered their favorite dishes without their ordering. Lane seemed to lighten up and spoke of nothing problematic. Most of the conversation was about Chad's reaction to the motor home.

Usually they were so satiated that dessert was out of the question. But tonight, for some mysterious reason, Paoli had insisted. Having removed everything except the candle and Barolo glasses, he pompously placed a gleaming silver-covered compote at Cass's place and scurried away. Not knowing how to react, Cass raised questioning eyebrows to Lane. He simply nodded and reached to remove the cover, his expressive eyes not leaving Cass's face. On a pad of royal blue velvet rested a huge sparkling diamond solitaire and a card with Lane's inimitable block printing, "Will you marry me?"

Cass was in total shock. This was the surprise of her

life. She barely realized that her favorite music, Beethoven's "Moonlight Sonata," was playing softly in the background. With trembling fingers, she reached for the ring and raised her glistening eyes to Lane's. His eyes were brimming, too.

"Yes, oh yes, my love, I will marry you. Please, you place it on my finger. It's the most beautiful ring I have ever seen in my entire life!" Cass murmured, breathlessly.

Lane lovingly placed the ring on her finger; then, without dropping her hand, he managed to maneuver to her side of the booth; he pulled her to her feet and crushed her against him.

"My beautiful, tender Cassandra, my life has just begun, because I love you so very, very much."

A completely unexpected and riotous celebration momentarily exploded. Paoli and his family, as well as the customers still present, were cheering, clapping, and wishing them the best. The patrons had been quietly informed of what to do as soon as Paoli gave them the thumbs-up signal.

"This calls for champagne for all! Bring out the Dom Perignon, Mamma, and let's toast to the happiness of our very dear friends!"

The Beethoven was quickly changed to some cherished 1940's dance favorites, the tables and chairs in the center were removed, making a cozy dance floor, and the impromptu engagement party proceeded with Paoli's proud supervision.

"Don't worry about the drive home, Dr. Lane, relax and celebrate. You have won your most beautiful and precious lady." And with a big hug for Cassio, "My breath nearly stopped while waiting to see which way your head would move when Dr. Lane removed the cover from that dish. You relax, too, Cassio. The Corvette is safely parked in my garage, and a cabbie is standing by to deliver you to whatever your destination will be later." All this with an impish grin.

Cass was whirled from one partner to another, some whom she recognized from previous visits, and some, total strangers. The dances were constantly interrupted at booth after booth by those who insisted on personal good wishes and close inspection of the glittering diamond. Cass was overwhelmed with the sincerity of everyone involved. Deeply she yearned for the peace and quiet of Lane's apartment and the safe harbor of his arms, but did not have the heart to quash the exuberance of a true Italian celebration, even though she knew that it would continue long after their departure. It had been a very long day, and she knew that Lane would graciously arrange their escape. Each time that she was taken back to his arms, he nuzzled her ear and whispered, "We will be alone very soon, Madam Queen." She secretly hoped that her nickname would never be turned into Ma Damn Queen, but could not help giggling at that thought.

Finally just as he had promised, Paoli poured them into a waiting cabbie's vehicle. In the front seat, he placed a basket overflowing with fruit packed around two more magnums of champagne. "Come back to see us very soon, my friends."

24

The next few weeks of scheduling problems were certainly not top priority for tonight. Thankfully, they had all day tomorrow for serious stuff. Lane's apartment was warm, cozy, and inviting. He dropped the fruit and champagne basket in the breakfast nook and engulfed Cass in his arms.

"All the ropes that have kept me hanging have just been cut loose. I do love you more every day, Cass," he whispered.

She unraveled from his embrace and purred.

"I'm going to get rid of some of these excess clothes while you light the fireplace, and then I want lots of slow soft kisses that will last forever." She then disappeared into the bedroom. Having no attire of her own, she searched for one of Lane's silk pajama tops—yes, the blue one; that always turned him on.

When she reappeared, Lane had the champagne and strawberries arranged on a silver tray in front of a blazing fire and lots of huge, soft, multicolored pillows tossed about on her favorite, massive, polar bear rug.

"Come to me, love of my life. We are curtailed to one glass of bubbly and one berry before we roll on the rug for some heavy loving. I want to kiss you all over until my tongue has stroked you senseless."

Between sips, Cass teasingly opened the buttons of his shirt and nuzzled. Somehow, the shirt was cast aside with the jeans, skivvies, and all else following quickly, leaving them expectantly together. Her nipples were as rosy as pink pearls as he laved them with his tongue. She combed her fingers through his thick, curly hair as he gently entered her while she massaged him with the walls of her vagina, releasing and contracting the muscles in an undulating motion that reduced him to a quivering male animal. They soared together on waves of ecstasy, lifting higher to a mind-jarring, blinding release, her body trembling from head to foot, the center of her sexual being exploding and spinning into a vortex of shattering orgasms. The raging beat of Lane's heart nearly drowned the sound of his moaning climax as he collapsed, his body quivering with seismic intensity.

"Madam Queen," he gasped, "our love far surpasses everything that ever existed. What a lot of our lives we have wasted not knowing of this love that we now have. Do we have the strength to have one more sip before we put another log on the fire and just cuddle?"

"Oh, Lane, my dearest love, I had no idea that such sensations existed. Let's bypass more champagne and just be close. I don't want to come down from my cloud just yet. There are still multicolored lights sending me toward earth on an iridescent rainbow. Just hold me, please?" Wrapped in each other's arms, they slept.

The sun's brilliant rays announced a clear morning as they shone upon the half-filled goblets. Cass awoke to find Lane on one elbow adoringly consuming her with his eyes.

"Whose turn is it to cook breakfast? It can't be mine 'cause coffee stains are hard to remove from blue silk, and that's all I have."

"Okay, Madam Queen, I will take that responsibility while you take notes on the list of projects that we have to face soon. Number one is the date that you must set for our wedding. Next is how we are going to convince Chad that spending a few weeks in Florida during this season (including Disneyland) with Tommy as his guest, *then* Alaska in the spring makes more sense. Number three, if we are staying at Amy's we must decide what to do with your home and my apartment, rent or sell. Number four, we must arrange for a caretaker at Amy's if we winter in Florida and summer in Alaska. Five, is to set in motion early retirement plans for me and notification at the hospital and private patients of my decision. Number six is setting up Chad's therapy and study schedule and, very important, keeping track of the status of the search for Archer."

The mention of Archer momentarily stunned Cass into deafening silence.

"Lane, are you certain that you want my problem cluttering your life?" she murmured, breathlessly. "I shall never give up. You must know that. Archer will always hold a special niche in my heart that no one else will ever occupy. It is a piece of the puzzle in my life that must be filled in before I can be completely at peace. I need to be certain that there'll be no negatives which might eventually tear us apart."

"My beautiful and lovely Cassandra, please eat your breakfast, and rest assured that all of your future I promise to willingly share. You will always have my support, as I want to make the search for Archer a prime project in my life as well. I want to spend the rest of my life very close to you, but in order to do that, we must make some definite plans. I cannot risk losing the love of my life, you, my reason for being, so please let's set a wedding date."

"Oh, Lane, my dearest, it cannot be too soon. Christmas is my favorite holiday, so let's plan to be married on Christmas Eve. And what about at Amy's home with just those closest to us. Chad wants to be part of our life, and Amy would love it, I'm certain. She will be leaving the day after Christmas in order to get settled in her new quarters during the holiday break at the Sorbonne. Chad must be at the hospital on December twenty-seventh for final release procedures, and we can have our honeymoon right at Amy's. I would love that."

"Agreed, Madam Queen, but how about an extended honeymoon touring the southern climes?"

"But what about Alaska? Chad does have his heart set on that trip," Cass gasped, with eyes as big as ferris wheels.

"I know, Cass, but if we explain to him the weather conditions, especially after last night, the extensive driving, and the places we couldn't see and the things we couldn't do, like chasing the buffalo herds in Saskatchewan during the winter months, he will agree. Particularly when we emphasize Disneyland, Sea World, Alligator Farms, Busch Gardens, plus extended hours fishing and relaxing on warm, sandy beaches, he will welcome the change. I also want your input on taking his friend at the hospital, Tommy, with us. I feel sure that the orphanage would agree that this is what Tommy needs as well as the rest of us. He would be a welcome and delightful companion for Chad as well as benefit from the therapy of weeks in the sunshine.

"On our return trip, we can take in Chincoteague, off the coast of Virginia, to watch the wild pony roundup. *That* they would never forget and neither would we. I have wanted to do that ever since I read *Misty of Chincoteague* when I was in the sixth grade. Do you know the story of Misty? Let's leave the dishes and lie by the fire while I tell you of one of my childhood fantasies. Later, while I'm preparing dinner, we can go on with our project list."

The telling of his childhood dream lulled Cass into a warm feeling of complete security, and she agreed that his plans were not only sensible but exciting.

"I will totally agree with your solution to problem

number one on one condition, that right now, we retire to your king-sized bed. Truly, it is more comfortable than the rug, and besides, the fire is dying."

"Done deal, my shameless wench." He laughed exultantly and scooping her up like a child, swept her to his bedroom. He pulled her close, while she pressed closer, reaching out with exploring hands to caress him and stroke his hard masculinity. Totally aroused in exquisite agony, he took her, loving her as she had never been loved before. Their passions completely spent, their exhaustion led them into a long and dreamless sleep.

It was dusk when Cass awoke, finding Lane awake and adoringly hovering over her.

"This is beyond crazy, but wonderful." Her eyes misted over as she pulled his face down to her lips. As they held each other, alone with their thoughts, his stomach growled, and Cass giggled.

"Okay, it's chow time for sure."

He got up from the rumpled bed and put on his robe as Cass sat unsteadily on the edge. He passed her the blue satin pajama top and supported her until her strength returned, then walked her out to the nook, brought out the remaining Dom Perignon, and carefully filled two flutes. It was time to prepare dinner.

25

A glistening dawn broke on December fourth. Cass and Lane rode in a cab through what looked like acres of diamonds to pick up the Corvette at Paoli's. Lane was thoroughly motivated.

"We have just twenty days to accomplish our goals, but we can do it. Before we talk to Chad, let's stop at Dr. Bob Holloway's office at the hospital. He is chairman of the board of trustees at Tommy's orphanage, and I'm certain that he will approve of our plans to take Tommy with us. He can call a special meeting of the board and put the plan into action. Thankfully, he knows both of us well and will welcome a chance like this for Tommy. If he says that it is a go, then we can include that in our explanation of changes to Chad."

"Okay, then we'll give Chad another day off from his formal classes. I can give him some homework, but with all this on his mind, it will probably be an exercise in futility. Then shall we take The Chariot to Amy's, where we can leisurely pack what we think we will need? Before we talk to Chad, shouldn't we call Amy and drop the bomb? She will approve, I know. That way, she will surely be at home. We really don't have time to shovel my car out of where it is no doubt buried, so shall I follow you in the Vette?"

"Good thinking! In that way, Amy will know what to expect. We'll have everything catered, and Amy's sound system can supply all the music we need. What do you think of Bob Holloway being my best man?"

"Oh, hon, that's a prime idea. He has been a close friend of yours for so long, and he dearly loves both of the boys. That plus the fact that Amy knows him and seems to have enjoyed his company in the past will add to the festivities. She will probably have to compete with my girlfriends for his attentions. Sue, Pat, Sybil, and Enid are the only ones whom I plan to invite. They have suffered through all my problems with me, so I must let them share the greatest happiness of my life."

"Agreed. And they obviously all love a party and can keep Bob on his toes—not necessarily on his best behavior, but on his toes. We will call them from Amy's, okay? Is Amy going to be your matron of honor?"

"Very definitely. She and the boys must be part of the ceremony, don't you think? Chad and Tommy can both be ring bearers somehow."

Chad and Tommy saw the Vette drive by, headed for the parking lot.

"Boy, I thought it would take them longer than this to get out from under those snow banks. I wish Cass would let you study with me, at least this week, 'cause next week is Christmas vacation anyway."

Tears welled in Tommy's eyes, but he turned away so that Chad would not see them. He did have friends at the orphanage. After all, he had spent his whole life there, and for ten years they had been his only family. But that big lump in his throat was because he had grown to love Chad like the brother that he never had and he dreaded the parting, especially at Christmas. That was supposed to be a family holiday, and he had no family. He would miss Chad and probably cry a lot but would have to get through it somehow. He knew that he would see Chad only when he had to return for periodic checkups. It was a deep down ache that he had carried ever since he knew of Chad's release sometime before Christmas.

Being highly sensitive to his best friend's feelings,

Chad had to try to keep his spirits up, at least for right now.

"They will be a while checking in at Lane's office, so let's at least start a game of Scrabble." He knew that it was Tommy's favorite game, and he was a formidable opponent.

Dr. Bob Holloway was just arriving when Cass and Lane appeared at his door.

"What glad tidings do you bring on such a gorgeous morning? I need some positive thoughts because I'd rather be skiing, but duty calls for all of us, right? Let's have some fresh coffee and relax before we face the troops. You two are emitting some pretty strong colorful auras. What are you up to?"

Cass could contain herself no longer. She dearly loved Bob and had to share their happiness with someone soon. Running across the room, she gave Bob a big hug, then stepped back and held both his hands.

"Bob, we are going to be married Christmas Eve," she burst out, "and we want you for best man. Please?" Lane stood back, grinning from ear to ear.

"Whoa! My two favorite people are taking the plunge? There could possibly be no better news." He shook Lane's hand, then gave Cass a warm, totally enveloping bear hug. "Congratulations, buddy! You can count on me. I wouldn't miss that for anything, even skiing. When? Where? How soon?"

Cass was bubbling with joy. She and Lane intermittently disclosed their plans.

"It's short notice, Bob, is this going to upset your holiday plans?"

"No way, my man, it just so happens with the schedule here, I am slotted to stay in the area. And this is a welcome invitation that I will more than look forward to.

Do I dare ask whether there will be any single chicks there?"

"Yes, four of my closest friends, who will keep you well entertained. They are all different types, no drones. Be prepared to be overwhelmed," Cass giggled.

"Now that we have you motivated for that part of the plans, we have another favor to ask of utmost importance." Lane explained what they needed in order to take Tommy with them for the summer and following winter.

Having treated both boys for the past weeks, Bob knew of the bond that had cemented between Chad and Tommy.

"That would, without a doubt, be the highlight of poor Tommy's life. He needs a family atmosphere right now, and certainly, no one would refuse him that chance. Let me make one phone call right now, which should firm up those plans. I will call a special board meeting for tonight to make everything legal and start the paper work for the records."

Cass was breathless.

"Are you that certain? We are on our way to Chad right now to announce our surprises, and we wouldn't want to get his hopes up about Tommy if it isn't a sure bet."

Dr. Bob Holloway made the phone call, nodding all the while in the affirmative.

"It's a go! You can count on it! And you are going to tell the boys today, I hope. They will be ecstatic; we all know that they have both dreaded being separated. In fact, I don't want to miss their faces when you tell them. Would it be invading your plans if I go up to Chad's room with you? If Tommy isn't already there, we will collect him. What a great present for both of them."

Cass folded her elbow in his arm.

"Let's do it. Let's go right now. Or should I call Amy

first? We have to go there sometime today, so let's share our plans with her, because she is deeply involved, too."
Amy answered the phone on the second ring.
"Hi, Cass, what's happening?"
"Amy, you have to know right now. It all just happened yesterday. Lane and I are going to be married, hopefully at your home on Christmas Eve, and please, will you be my matron of honor?" Cass was so emotional and choked up that she was having a hard time talking. "Lane wants to talk with you, okay?"
"Hi, Amy, are you stunned? May we come to the house this afternoon and leave the motor home with you for the time being? Chad won't be with us today, but we are on the way to his room right now. We can't wait to share our plans with him."
"Yes! Yes! Of course! Congratulations and all that stuff. Are you changing your plans re Alaska? I can't believe you two and can't wait to see you. Plan on having dinner here, okay?"
"Now to Chad's room. Forward." Bob Holloway led the way.

26

Chad heard Lane's voice in the corridor and made a mad dash for the door, tripping on the leg of the game table and landing flat on his face, leaving Tommy madly attempting to keep the table upright. After all, he was finally ahead in the game. Quickly helping Chad to his feet, Lane saw that Chad was not hurt in any way, other than his pride.

"Hey, Buddy, I've never before been greeted like a high Eastern Pooh-Bah, on your knees with forehead to the floor. Have you been practicing that routine very long?"

"Aw, Cass, he's picking on me again. Hi, Doc Holloway. Shall I try it again for you and Cass?" Everyone was grinning.

"We have arrived with an unsuspected surprise, guys. Lane and I are engaged to be married and wanted you to be the first to share our happiness." Cass flashed her diamond.

"Wow! Where do you carry the battery? I've never seen a ring as huge as that before," Tommy gushed.

"Isn't it magnificent? And now let us try to explain our change in plans. Alaska is on the back burner for now, but . . ." Chad's jaw dropped and his face paled. "But we are only stalling that trip until spring and replacing those plans to head for Florida first."

Tommy was trying to quietly sidle toward the door. He saw Chad's disappointment, and he wasn't sure that he wanted to hear the plans. It was only two weeks till Christmas, and he knew that he would be alone at the orphanage again. And he for sure didn't want them to see him crying.

"See you later, I gotta go."

Bob Holloway caught Tommy and lifted him off the floor.

"What do you mean you gotta go? You can't leave now, my good friend, because you are a big part of these plans!"

"Me? Aw, c'mon."

Chad was speechless. Had he heard right? He grabbed Cass's wrist.

"What does he mean, Cass?"

Cass engulfed Chad in her arms.

"Just what he said. Tommy and you are going to be part of our wedding on Christmas Eve at Amy's. Isn't that great? And Doc Holloway will be our best man and—"

Tommy leaped to the edge of the bed and put his arms around Chad.

"They mean it! They mean it! I can't believe that I don't have to say good-bye to you yet. Oh, my gosh, thank you so very much. But will the orphanage let me go, Doc Holloway?"

"You can bet they will. I have already started the paperwork flowing, so don't give that another thought. You are going."

"But I don't have any wedding clothes, Cass."

"You will have, Tommy, and be totally rigged out for Florida and Alaska."

"Florida and Alaska, too, in The Chariot with Chad? I must be dreaming."

"Nope," Lane added, "we really need you with us, then Chad won't have to take care of two dogs. Each one of you will have the total, and I do mean total, care, feeding, exercising, bathing, et cetera, of Millie and Nell. You two will have to flip a coin on which dog is whose responsibility. And now, Cass has two students to keep up to par on schoolwork. So you see, each one of us has responsibilities."

"Now we are on our way to Amy's to share our plans," Cass added. "You guys had better start making a list of what you want to take, like your favorite Nintendo games, videos, cassette tapes, et cetera. Don't worry about clothes. Santa Claus will take care of that. Oh, what size Nikes do you wear? Santa can figure out the rest. And try to remember the seasoned traveler's motto, 'Pack all you think you want, then remove at least half of it.' You two have a lot of decisions to make, right?"

"Gee, right, we'll start today," in unison, and there were good-bye hugs.

"It's a good thing you two are just across the hall from each other," Cass giggled. "I suspect there will be a bit of traffic tonight. You will miss looking at The Chariot for awhile because we are taking it to Amy's today, . . . so get cracking and we'll see you tomorrow."

As Dr. Bob Holloway, Cass, and Lane walked down the corridor, they could hear the boys. "Oh, Tommy, wait'll you see the TV, VCR and all the other electronic gear Lane has in The Chariot!"

"Awesome," was all Tommy could say.

As Cass and Lane cleared the snow from the motor home, two dark-haired little ten-year-old boys were pressing their noses against the window, watching it all in complete amazement. Just as the snow removal was finished, Chad couldn't resist. He raised the window and shouted, "Do we have to wear neckties at the wedding?"

27

The convoy back to Dr. Amy Fielding's home in Wellesley was fun, with Cass following The Chariot in Lane's Corvette. The CBs were active all the way.

"Gotcha ears on, Voo Doo Chile?"

"That's an affirmative, Medic, we are on our way! Shall we let Chad and Tommy pick their own handles for our trip?"

"Sure," crackled Medic's voice, "they will love that, but we can suggest."

A new voice cropped up.

"Hey, Voo Doo Chile, are you the chick snugged up behind the big Pace Arrow RV, pushing a real sporty GM product? That's real class, but what's happening? Are you trying to save gas by being pulled along in the RV's vacuum? This is Tiger Cat in the eighteen wheeler right behind you. Looks like Medic and I have you in the rocking chair."

"Right, Tiger Cat," Lane broke in on that comment, "this is Medic. We are traveling in tandem. Voo Doo keeps a pretty straight wake, right?"

"You're a lucky gent, Medic, she's real class. Apologies for attempting to move in on your territory, but nothing ventured, nothing gained," chuckled Tiger Cat. "It's unusual seeing a real muscle car like that poking along at the legal speed limit. The last one I followed was Supreme Court Justice Charles Thomas's. At the time, he was pushing a 1990 Corvette ZR1. Man, that has 420 horse power. I wrote his license plate down to have someone translate." Tiger Cat spelled out "R E S I P S A. It's a Latin phrase, meaning 'it speaks for itself.' Clever, huh?"

"Thanks for the fun rap, Tiger Cat. Have a safe trip, and watch out for those bubblegum machines!"

"Affirmative, Medic, take good care of Voo Doo Chile and keep your powder dry."

Cass had not become involved in that exchange. All she could do was giggle.

"Fun, huh, Voo Doo?" was Medic's next comment.

"I love it, but I'm glad that I'm not alone. His voice was really sexy."

"Wow. This is Tiger Cat's one last word. Thanks, Voo Doo. I'll pass on by with that compliment. You've made my day." He waved and touched his air horn on the way by.

Following the phone call from Cass, Amy wandered from window to window with mixed emotions, the dogs close at her heels. Her first reaction was that this was the best thing that could have happened to both of them. Cass needed a stable trusting relationship, and certainly Lane would never let her down. He had needed love in his life for some time, and Cass would spend the rest of her life devoted to him. Amy totally approved of their marriage and was not surprised that they were including both Chad and Tommy in their immediate plans. She could be completely at ease leaving Chad in their care while she was in Europe. Who knew where it would go from there? Should she share the final news of Archer just yet? No, she would figure out a way to break the news when the time was right. Let them enjoy their trip to Florida at least.

It would be great to see Bob Holloway again. He would be fun at the wedding. Too bad that she would have so much competition from all of Cass's single girlfriends.

Amy had always found Dr. Holloway attractive, but was a little shy about approaching one of the most popular bachelors in the area. She must perish those thoughts. Just because Cass had found her mate, why should she be thinking along those lines. Probably it was a good thing that her plans were firm. But she could dream, couldn't she?

Amy could not help but smile as her thoughts drifted toward her first appointments with Cassandra, who was so bitter and hurt. She recalled her opinion of the only answer to a successful, monogamous, trusting, sincere, and long-lasting relationship with a male was to get another cocker spaniel. Lane had certainly turned her life around, thankfully. She would have fun reminiscing with Cass at some later date.

Time could not pass fast enough for Amy. It was more than helpful that the wedding plans would keep her busy, plus her own packing for her flight out of Logan Airport on the day after Christmas. Sleeping quarters would be no problem on Christmas Eve and Christmas night. The boys could share Chad's room. Bob Holloway she would put in the den which had its own bath facilities. The bride and groom could have the separate guest quarters to themselves.

Still wandering from room to room, her thoughts skittered from one subject to another. Would she feel lonely traveling alone? There would be nobody at Orly Airport in Paris to greet her, but at least she had an apartment to go to, and her conversational French was passable, so she should be all set. Would Nell and Millie miss her? No, Chad and Tommy would keep them too busy. Would she have trouble keeping her research in focus with Bob Holloway fading in and out of her consciousness? She would surely have to concentrate. After all, studying was her reason for going to the Sorbonne.

Just don't get sidetracked, kiddo.

The dogs raced to the door as The Chariot drove in, followed by the Vette. With hugs, kisses, tears, and congratulations, the three were talking all at once.

"First of all, Amy, tell me where you want The Chariot parked, out of your way. It will be here for a couple of weeks, and we really appreciate it," Lane expounded. "It will be so much easier to get all our gear stowed properly." Lane maneuvered The Chariot into place, and Cass and Amy retired to the breakfast nook.

"Let's have lunch first and then call the girls about our plans. Does Lane have a minister in mind, Cass?"

"Really, he is so efficient and knows so many people. He is going to call the Aleppo Shrine Temple chaplain, who lives right here in Wellslay. Isn't that great?"

"That's perfect. Now let's decide on a caterer, both for the Christmas Eve wedding dinner and the turkey for Christmas, okay? Knowing Bob and Lane, they will have taken care of all the champagne and stuff, right?"

"I'm sure of that. Can you believe all this, Amy? Everything is moving so fast, but I will never be more certain of anything in my life that we are doing the right thing. I do love Lane so much."

"She is no surer than I am, Amy," Lane said as he snuggled into the nook beside Cass and grinned. "I cannot believe that I have found the girl of my dreams, the love of my life, my Madam Queen."

"Okay, you two love birds, let's munch down then get on the phones. Cass, you take the line in my office for your calls to the girls, and Lane, you can sit right here when you are ready to contact the chaplain. I will take care of the caterer, the Christmas tree, and the flowers later, okay?"

"That's perfect, Amy. Meanwhile, I'll do the shopping

for the boys. No doubt they need everything in the clothes department from the skin out. I told them that Santa Claus would take care of all that for them," Cass added.

"Then we'll also give them money envelopes for their fun cash on the trip south. That should about do it," sighed Lane. "Now let's get on the phones so Amy can have some time to herself. We do have to return tonight, you know. What are you wearing for the wedding?"

Shrieks from both.

"That's our secret, Lane, you're not supposed to know."

28

Those twenty days between four and twenty-four of December were packed with details of the wedding, Lane's retirement, decisions regarding his apartment as well as rental of Cass's home, retaining a dependable caretaker for Amy's residence, checking on definite travel routes, and packing The Chariot. Chad and Tommy were released from the hospital on the twenty-second, and Cass moved in with Amy along with the boys to the great delight of Millie and Nell.

The wedding day, December twenty-fourth, was heaven-sent, perfect weather. The boys were thrilled that they had been placed in total charge of decorating the Christmas tree, another new experience for Tommy. His comment, "Awesome," was becoming almost his mantra.

The Coleman sleeping bags were presents given to the boys early on. Each had his own name embroidered and a note saying that they had permission to sleep in The Chariot until the trip if they wished. There was no question of their decision, looking forward to all the privacy and hours to plan way into the night. Their list of "things to see" had already been submitted to Cass and Lane, but they reviewed it to be very certain not to miss anything. It was in those hours that they also made their decision for the future. Chad was going to West Point; therefore, his CB handle would be Pointer. Tommy couldn't imagine being separated from Chad, so his fantasy was harder to grasp. For the time being and realizing that he had lots of years ahead, he chose Annapolis and liked the handle of Commodore. Those choices would be all the more interesting when they visited both sites in New York and Maryland, either on the way to Florida or on the return trip. They hoped that Santa Claus would include cameras on his list. Lane already had a Sony camcorder.

The wedding plans advanced exceptionally smoothly, a symphony in blue as the chaplain tagged it. Cass wore a sky-blue, tailored ensemble, Amy's a bit darker blue. Lane and Bob wore navy blue suits, while Chad and Tommy preened in their blue blazers, lighter blue trousers, and white turtlenecks. Sue was in total charge of the camcorder; Sybil was everywhere with her Olympus zoom-lens camera; Enid supervised the bar; and Pat checked and rechecked on the caterer's food planning and serving. Lane and Bob surpervised the wine for dinner and the Dom Perignon for the wedding toasts, as well as the appropriate music for the sound system. The wedding dinner was an artistic buffet and thoroughly enjoyed by all.

Amy was astounded but highly flattered that Bob Holloway was so attentive. She really didn't want to blame it on the wine and champagne. It did figure that if the bubblies were the reason for his being at her shoulder constantly, he would certainly be flirting with all the other single gals, especially Sue and Sybil. They were so much fun and so very sophisticated. At least they had agreed on Pat as the "designated driver".

By eight-thirty P.M., the girls had left with congratulatory hugs all around and best wishes for a successful trip, assured that they would receive cards now and then. The chaplain had left soon after dinner after blessing them all individually. The boys escaped to their lair in The Chariot, having promised that they would exercise Millie and Nell and would not be late in the morning for the Christmas tree. The caterers had cleared all signs of the buffet dinner and promised to be there for preparation of the dinner at one o'clock on Christmas day.

Needless to say, everyone was close to exhaustion, but Cass, Lane, Amy, and Bob decided on a quiet nightcap, just the four of them, finally. Cass had never felt so loved and secure. One nightcap led to two. Then Lane announced that tomorrow would be an early and busy day. With his shy, inimitable grin, he raised one eyebrow and winked at Cass. It had been some time since Cass had blushed, but she gracefully escaped, collecting the brandy snifters, quickly saying, "Good night, you two, see you early in the morning."

It was around three A.M. when Lane awoke exceptionally thirsty. He could quietly raid the kitchen refrigerator for ice cubes and return without waking Cass. Passing by the den, there was no Bob Holloway. He didn't need to check his whereabouts, because Amy's bedroom door was closed, which never happened, but it was closed now. *Great,* thought Lane, *they finally have a chance to be alone. I just hope that it will develop into a commitment. No one could be as ecstatically happy and contented as I am right now, and I want the same for Amy and Bob. True, she's leaving on the twenty-sixth, but a continent away would not deter Bob Holloway.*

The next morning Chad and Tommy had managed to very quietly exercise the dogs and, without a rattle, had fed them in the kitchen. They were found in the living room, dressed in their brilliant-colored sweat suits, sitting and staring wide-eyed at all the wrapped gifts. Millie was resting beside Tommy, who had assumed a very proprietary attitude toward her. With the renowned and amusing logic of ten-year-olds, the boys had decided that because Tommy had ems in his name, Millie would be his responsibility. Chad was just thankful that Nell had seemed to adopt him. There was not a whisper between them, only pantomined signals, pointing first at one package and then another with raised eyebrows. They dared not get close enough to read the name tags.

"Good morning and merry Christmas, Mr. and Mrs. Hamilton," chided Bob as he appeared in the doorway of the den.

Lane grinned, but only the two men knew why.

"Hopefully, we are going to forego a big breakfast with Christmas dinner on the schedule. And besides, these two rascals have waited long enough to see what Santa Claus has left. Right?"

"Agreed," echoed Cass. "Are you two going to pass out the gifts? Hi, Amy. Merry Christmas. We really wouldn't have started without you. There's coffee, juice, and hot cocoa on the kitchen counter after each one has opened one gift, okay? Tommy, you're first because you are closest."

"Awesome," Tommy sighed.

29

Chad and Tommy were overwhelmed with their gifts, everything they had dreamed of plus things that hadn't even occurred to them. Each had innumerable summer outfits, all with their name tags. Their Nike running shoes were a perfect fit, but the cameras in leather cases with extra film topped their highest expectations.

"I just wish that I could say thank you in at least fourteen different languages," said Tommy as he and Chad hugged the adults before cleaning up the Christmas paper and ribbons.

"Guess we'd better clear the decks, pack our gear in The Chariot, and exercise Nell and Millie, hadn't we, Lane?" Chad was now anxious to get on the road.

"Right, guys, the caterers will be here with dinner preparations any minute, so let's keep out of their way."

The Christmas turkey, and all that went with it, was served promptly at four P.M. The Chariot had been plugged into the electricity, so it was agreed to put all leftovers into that refrigerator for munchies during their trip.

During dinner, Amy had shyly announced that Bob Holloway wanted to take her to the airport in the morning. It would be extremely early, so they had better share their parting thoughts before they retired for the night.

With twinkling eyes and his infectious chuckle, Bob added to Amy's comments.

"You know, Lane, I've decided that your decision to retire early is a smart one, and I plan to do the same very shortly. There is no way that I can relax, knowing that Amy is alone in Paris. For sure, she won't be alone for long, but I should be nearer than a continent away to face any competition, right?"

"Bob, what a great idea! I won't worry about her nearly so much if you are there." Cass was totally sincere on that basis but smiled widely when she added, "But that competition works both ways, so keep an eye on *him,* Amy."

At five A.M. the day after Christmas, the boys quietly fed Nell and Millie and made fresh orange juice for everybody's travel mugs. They had all agreed to have breakfast at a rest stop on the way. Everyone was too excited to eat anyway, and by six thirty A.M., everything was go—the house secured, one last call to the caretaker, and they were on their way.

Chad and Tommy pored studiously over the Triptik and maps that had been prepared, with West Point and Annapolis circled. Beyond that, they were not certain what they should be watching for.

Cass was deliriously happy riding shotgun, as the boys called it. She could not keep her eyes off Lane's chiseled profile. He was so much in command and never failed when the opportunity arose to mouth the words, "I love you, Madam Queen."

Lane announced that they would be stopping the first night in the Newburgh, New York, area on Route 84-West, which many seasoned RV owners had advised. With pit stops on the way, he judged that they would be off the highway long before dark. The next day, they should be well rested for the scenic route, 9-W, which would take them directly to The West Point Military Academy and Fort Montgomery. Lane also decided that a 76 Truck Stop would be their best bet for the first night. Those truck stops were always secure, and the boys would be thrilled meeting and chatting with friendly truckers. Chad and Tommy couldn't believe that the truckers who pulled mobile homes could be arrested for even a night light on the mobile home protruding just an inch and a half beyond the width limit.

It was astounding to them the number of rules and regulations the truckers had to know, all different in each state. They were wide-eyed as they listened to the advice about where the cop traps were and major constructions to avoid. The truckers' suggestions to leave their CB radios on for information, plus guaranteed amusement was well recorded by the boys. Chad and Tommy were thrilled to share their CB handles. Who knew, they might be talking to the same truckers going the same route. They were sure to write down all the CB handles that were shared and what vehicle they were pushing. Their favorite new friend was Paul Whiteman from upstate New York, known as King Paul. He promised to keep an eye out for them south of Maryland.

Their tour of West Point was beyond all expectation, leaving Chad totally convinced that he would do all in his power to be a graduate of that renowned institution. Tommy began to waiver on his decision of Annapolis, but stated that he would reserve his firm opinion until after they toured the naval academy.

It was fun at all the rest stops. There were so many RVs headed south from many of the northeastern states and the Canadian provinces. They all took turns using the restrooms and walking the dogs. On one visit Tommy lost control of his usually well-modulated voice.

"Will you take a look at what's riding on the dashboard of that big Southwind motor home over there!" he shrieked. "It's a real live fox! Wow, I've never even seen a real live fox before. Awesome!" Another traveling pet was a playful monkey whose owners were delighted to share its antics with the boys.

"We'd better start writing smaller or our notebooks

are going to be filled before we get south of the Mason-Dixon line," offered Chad.

"Gotcha! You think that I don't know that we've already done that, huh? The Mason-Dixon line is the boundary between Pennsylvania and Maryland, surveyed by Charles Mason and Jeremiah Dixon from 1763 to 1767. It was regarded as the line between the North and South during the Civil War, right?" chattered Tommy. Chad vowed that he would trick him yet.

Both Lane and Cass's eyebrows went straight up to their hairlines.

"Sakes, Tommy," offered Cass. "You certainly get an A-plus on that history lesson. Is that your favorite subject?"

"Not really. I guess I'm called a Civil War buff. Chad is more into World War Two, so he'll outgrade me on that subject. I thought about Gettysburg but knew it was way off our route."

"It won't be on the return trip, Tommy. We've made definite plans for that. Cass and I have never been there either, so don't cross it off your list," advised Lane.

After both tours, West Point and Annapolis, they were all anxious to head south for some warm beach weather. Their reservations were all made for the Kon Tiki Trailer Park on Crescent Beach, Route A1A, in St. Augustine, Florida. They had a choice location, right on the beach, with only one RV on their left. The front view and right side were open to the ocean and sand dunes—lots of privacy.

30

Each night throughout their traveling, Cass tucked the boys' sleeping bags around them and kissed them good night after hearing their prayers. She always silently included Archer in hers. Would she ever find him? Somewhere, did she have grandchildren of her own? As much as she was in love with Lane and overjoyed with her present life, Cass still kept Archer close to her heart. Was he still alive? Did he know the truth of his parentage? If he did, would he ever understand and forgive her? Were his adoptive parents capable of giving him the love that she held in her heart? Did he have adoptive brothers and sisters? If so, had he been treated any differently because he was adopted? Did he ever wonder about her?

So many, many questions bounced through her waking hours and in her dreams. If she found Archer, would Lane totally accept him? He had tried to assure Cass that he wanted and needed Archer, too. But what if Archer were a hippie, a druggie, a paraplegic, a homeless person, a convict, or . . . ? Sometimes her imagination ran rampant. There was always the question whether Archer would accept them as well. Even though Amy was in Europe, was the investigation still proceeding? In all the excitement of the past days, she had not mentioned this to Amy. It did seem strange that Amy had said nothing about Archer since she and Lane had announced their marriage plans. But her confidence that the results of Amy's efforts would eventually be forthcoming never lagged.

Her thoughts were not totally obsessive, and Cass was very careful not to let Lane know that Archer's presence was constant. Would Archer have loved McDonalds and Burger King as much as Chad and Tommy did? Was he the scholarly type in school? Had he ever been involved in athletics? Was he a leader or a follower? Was he an introvert or an extrovert? Was life easy for him? Had he been able to follow his dreams, or even been encouraged to do so? Had he been in the armed services? If so, was he one of the many missing-in-action veterans? Usually, Cass's thoughts were not negative, and when they did seep through, she promptly changed that avenue of thinking.

Would she ever share her hidden grief with Chad? Would he accept her tragic decision of giving her own baby up for adoption so many, many years ago? The questions were endless, especially when she was alone while Lane was on the beach, fishing or sight-seeing with the boys. Her lonely prayers for Archer's good fortune never ceased. Cass realized that her present circumstances sustained her sanity. Lane, Chad, and Tommy were her life now, and she loved them deeply. Tommy had no family at all. Could she allow him to be adopted by strangers? She must discuss this with Lane.

Each day, rain or shine, they all frolicked on the beach, and their sea shell collection became more and more interesting. The *Golden Book of Sea Shells* was their constant reference for identification. They had learned to be the first ones on the beach each morning to check whatever had washed ashore overnight. Always in the back of their minds was their planned visit to Sanibel Island, the sea shell capital of the world. Another field trip was going to be the beach at Venice on the West Coast, where they could sit in the waves at the water's edge and collect innumerable sharks' teeth.

Lane and the boys had collected dozens of Spanish bayonet branches to nail around the covered shelter beside The Chariot. They called it their South Sea island native hut, and indeed, it did have that appearance. There was a large table where their classes with Cass were held each day and even a double hammock. They had also retrieved huge blocks of tightly-packed coquina shells from the local state park to build a fire pit.

The park attendant had explained that coquina was Spanish for shellfish, which over long periods formed a soft, whitish natural limestone of broken shells and corals cemented together used in the southern United States for building. In fact, the famous local fort at Castillo de San Marcos had been totally built of coquina.

This was the subject of one of their most fascinating school lessons. They had listened carefully to the guide and took notes when visiting the fort and surprised Cass with a combined composition of its history after a few visits to the local library for their secret research. Theirs is the following essay, "The Fort Improvised from Golden Rock":

> The defenders of the outpost of St. Augustine were not very lucky with the wooden forts upon which they first relied. Those that were not burned down by attacking forces rotted in the humid climate.
>
> They had to find something more substantial, but as one Spanish officer put it, "There are no stones in the whole country." However, over on Anastasia Island there was a strange sort of rock that seemed to be made of seashells. Perhaps half a million years ago in the Pleistocene Age, a mollusk called Donat grew by the billions in the warm sea, forming vast shell layers that solidified into a mass mixed with sand and cemented with calcite from the shells themselves.
>
> The rocklike substance that resulted got its name from a Spanish word, that translated literally means shellfish or cockle and describes a little half inch butter-

fly clam that still washes up on Florida's shores, and incidentally makes a delicious broth.

The Spaniards discovered that masons could shape the substance with a carpenter's saw or an ax, but when exposed to the air the surface hardened. It was the answer to a fort builder's prayer, so it was decided that the city's new bastion would be built of this coquina rock and the project got underway in 1672. First a labor gang of peons and convicts, as well as one hundred and fifty unfortunate Indians who were dragooned into service, had to clear the palmetto and live-oak thickets from the deposits on Anastasia—no enviable task. No one knows how many fell victims to snakebite!

Once the rock was exposed, quarrymen from Havana chopped deep grooves into the soft yellow stone and cracked out slabs, which were hauled by oxcart to Escolta Creek and floated down on barges and across the Matanzas to the building site opposite the inlet.

The job of building the Castillo took twenty-nine years and cost so much money that Philip the Second moodily observed that the fort in the distant colony of Florida must have been built of solid silver. Even if it had been built of gold instead of the golden coquina, it was worth it because it kept Spain dominant in Florida in spite of British attacks.

When General Oglethorpe landed on Anastasia Island in 1740, he set up a battery of guns that could have shattered a granite or brick structure, but for thirty days his gunners pounded the Castillo in vain while the population of St. Augustine huddled inside the walls alternately starving and praying. One of the English artillerymen exclaimed in disgust, "What's the use? Our shots have no effect on San Marcos! Why, it's just like sticking a knife into a round of cheese."

Coquina became the principal material used in building. In addition to the Castillo, Fort Matanzas, which guards the inlet at the other end of Anastasia Island, was built of the golden stone, as well as the Cathedral, the oldest house, most of St. Augustine's public buildings and the finer homes of the citizens. Along the coast wherever coquina was available it was used. There are ruins of missions built of coquina to be found near Ormond and New Smyrna. In modern times the Bok Tower is perhaps the most notable structure built of coquina.

The quarries of Anastasia where the golden rock was obtained yielded still another dividend of gold. In the 1950's Aaron Dutton was exercising his dog near the water-filled coquina pits. The thirsty animal stopped to drink from the pool, and his master, looking down, saw that the water was literally alive with goldfish. It is surmised that the fish got there originally by the hands of a World War 2 service wife whose husband was suddenly reassigned. Having nothing else to do with her pet fish, she freed them in the waters of the coquina pits, where they multiplied madly.

In 1828 Spain turned East Florida over to the United States, but after the colorful ceremony at The Castillo de San Marcos, the soldiers of the 4th Regiment of Artillery, which was the town's first U.S. Army Garrison, were hard put to find quarters. Fort San Marcos housed them temporarily, since the St. Francis Barracks at the other end of town were in complete disrepair. The following year, in 1882, these barracks were renovated and the three companies of the 4th Artillery (121 men in all) took up permanent quarters there.

It was the old fort's turn to be neglected, since at that time it was held to be obsolete, although it went by the high-sounding title of Arsenal of East Florida. An unfortunate quartermaster officer, who was expected to live there, found that the only two rooms not being used for storage leaked badly, so he rented housing in town.

The renovators of St. Francis Barracks got the stone for a nice, new wharf by dismantling part of the sea wall near the fort. Though the breach of tides washed in threatening the fort and the town as well. The watchtowers began to crumble, there were large cracks in the walls, and the outworks leaned crazily into the encroaching sea. Finally in 1883 Congress appropriated $20,000 for repairs to the old fort (by then known as Fort Marion), and eventually a Lt. Stephen Tuttle was sent down to supervise the job. He lost no time in earning the enmity of the townspeople, who even in those days knew that the fort was an irreplaceable historic monument.

Lt. Tuttle had decided to use the money to rebuild the seawall instead, although he did make a few perfunctory repairs. While opening some closed rooms to clear out rubbish, he made the famous discovery of the human bones in the old gunpowder storage (the dungeon), which so many thousands of visitors have since bent their backs to see.

Lt. Tuttle was so unpopular that he was eventually taken off the job. A successor arrived to estimate the cost of both a new seawall and repairs of the fort, but it took Congress three more years to allocate the necessary funds.

The Army Engineers fought a series of problems in accomplishing their tasks, but the work was finally completed in 1842. Local citizens were still not too happy however, since Bay Street presented a rather sad spectacle. The government had done a good job on the seawall, but neglected to fill in Bay Street all the way out to it. At every flood tide the bay waters washed in behind the wall and remained for days in smelly, stagnant pools.

By the end of 1843, Fort Marion was in good shape and once more a functional bastion in the area's defense. The old Spanish seawall in front had been rebuilt and the moat filled in, providing a site for a powerful battery that commanded the harbor. Guns were mounted on the terreplein and the walls were repaired. When Florida became the twenty-seventh state of the Union, it was ready to be used in its defense.

Today, The Castillo de San Marcos stands as monument to Spain's influence in the Western hemisphere and to the early efforts of Europeans to carve out a foothold in wild and contested territory. From behind the ancient cannon visitors to the ancient fort can easily imagine the defenders of St. Augustine as they peered out toward the Gulf Stream in search of the pirates and corsairs that would sink their treasure-laden galleons or storm ashore to claim this strategically important piece of land.

Chad and Tommy certainly received an A-plus on that effort. After Cass had edited their project, corrected the spelling, and discussed sentence structure as a special language arts lesson, Cass assured them that they would make terrific public relations agents for the area.

31

Amy and Bob Holloway still sparked like downed electrical wires, even though it was so early in the morning. Their feelings on the trip to the airport were a mixture of anticipation of traveling to Paris and sorrow of separation. Bob had dreaded their parting and decided to suggest an alternate plan.

"Amy, is another twelve hours going to totally foul up your plans? I took it upon myself to check out another flight, and you could leave at 8:50 tonight, giving us another whole day together. I want to make love to you one more time before you leave, sweetheart. We can spend the whole day right here at the airport hotel, except for one hour that I need to do some very important, impromptu shopping."

His suggestion hit with all the intensity of an earthquake registering nine on the Richter scale. With the raging beat of her heart, Amy sighed.

"Yes. Yes, Bob. How can I refuse? I do want to be with you so much that it hurts. And besides, that TWA flight is direct with no changes involved. And it does make sense to arrive at the Charles De Gaulle airport in Paris at 9:30 in the morning rather than late at night. You see, I had considered that flight originally, but that was when I thought that I would be alone on the day after Christmas, and that would have been a deep emotional strain that I don't need. Handling loneliness is not my expertise."

"All right, my love, let's check in at the hotel, then I will go over to the TWA desk and make your necessary change of plans. Meanwhile, you can order a champagne breakfast for us, okay? Don't forget the Dom Perignon or the Moet et Chandon or whatever. Surprise me."

While Bob was on his mysterious errand, Amy arranged for breakfast for two. She couldn't help thinking how her life had changed—from the flatlands with no mountain peaks to a roller coaster because she had spirit enough to be bad, having realized that she had better make use of what Mother Nature had given her before Father Time took it away. She smiled as she thought of the advice she had given to so many of her clients, "Are you going to live the rest of your life lonely, troubled, and sad? No, you've got to live it up before you give it up."

Just thinking about Bob was like opening a bottle of champagne. Amy searched for words that might apply to him—curious, spontaneous, and overwhelming came to mind. With both feet planted firmly in midair, she called room service for the champagne. They would order breakfast later, when he returned, probably much later. The Dom Perignon was promptly delivered on ice, with one brilliant red rose in a sleek, crystal vase. How appropriate. They must have radiated with an aura of love when they checked in at the front desk.

In less than one hour, Bob returned, but it had seemed like eons. Glancing at the champagne, he grinned and placed an exotically wrapped tiny package beside the rose.

"Later, okay?"

His hand moved down her sides. One palm edged between their bodies until he stroked between her thighs. She quivered against his demands, her throbbing response strengthening until she had to grip his shirt to remain upright. When his fingers penetrated her, she opened her eyes in wide surprise. The pulsing increased, and Amy closed her eyes at last to the velvet darkness of passion. She climaxed against his hand, clinging to his

shoulders, crying into his shirt, shooting stars exploding. He held her tightly against him until the trembling abated, his hand still pressed to the moistness. When at last her breath gave her opportunity to speak, she whispered against his chest.
"I didn't know it could happen that way." His lips brushed her hair.
"The education of Amy Fielding has barely begun," he murmured. The promise of his words as vibrantly kept and carried out throughout the day.
It was difficult to part at the airport, but Bob promised to join her very soon. He had asked her to open her present only after her flight had departed. Free-living Dr. Robert Holloway, man of the world, man of experience; during takeoff, thoughts of him inflamed Amy nearly as much as his touch on Christmas Eve, and again today at the hotel. While still in sight of the airport, Amy opened the delicately beautiful package, revealing a little suede bag in the distinctive blue of Tiffany's. Inside was a bracelet made out of ropes of gold and silver entwined with a note, "What would I do without you!"
Amy knew that she had the administrator's gift; in the past, she could always reverse her opinions as the wind shifted and convince herself that she had never thought otherwise. But this time? Could she gain control? Would she ever really see Bob Holloway again? What did he *really* think of her? Had she been too easy? Having been a popular bachelor for so long, Bob had surely had many women. She could measure up to anyone in intelligence, but was she sophisticated enough? Could she hold his interest when the flames of their sexual encounters dwindled? Would there be any more of those? Bob had never mentioned a definite commitment. Would he pull well in double harness again? Would she? Those disturbing thoughts raced. Amy decided to direct her mind to an-

other subject or, at the rate she was going, her future would last about a week.

In the course of the day at the hotel, Amy had shared her knowledge of Archer's background with Bob. His welcomed advice regarding what to do with the final information seemed sound. All the final records of Archer were locked away in her safe. Bob's suggestion had been to leave them there until Cass, Lane, and the boys had at least returned from Florida, possibly after their Alaska trip. It was his feeling that he would like to discuss the situation with Lane before Cass had to be burdened with all the details. Why spoil their honeymoon. When they returned would be time enough to recover from such a shock.

32

The winter went much too fast in Florida. The whole state had been thoroughly explored—from Key West, where the boys were bug-eyed at the young girls with shaved heads and barefooted, and with their live, pet snakes draped around their shoulders, to the tour of the naval air station in Jacksonville. They missed nothing—Busch Gardens, Disneyworld, Sea World, sponge divers at Tarpon Springs, the cruise of Biscayne Bay, where the millionaires had their yachts tied up right at their own back door (Budweiser, Scott's tissue company, et cetera; they remembered the tour guide asking over the intercom how many each one of the passengers had invested in those yachts over the years).

Sanibel Island, the sea shell capital of the world, was one of their favorite visits, and so was picking up sharks' teeth on the beach at Venice. If they had to vote on only one favorite, it would have been extremely difficult. They could still not quite believe that they had attended the roundup of wild ponies off the coast of Virginia. Cass, as part of their tutoring, had been reading *Misty of Chincoteague* to them, as well as *Star, Son of Misty*.

The sight of wild horses of all ages swimming from Chincoteague to the mainland was another unforgettable experience. It did have its sad moments when the horses and colts were auctioned. Chad and Tommy both hoped and prayed that each one that was purchased would be treated well. They hated to see wild animals contained, but understood that cutting down the herd was necessary. And secretly, between them, they vowed that if either was able to own their own horse, this was where they would go for their purchase. The gift shop had replicas of Misty as well as other souvenirs of their visit. They bought a refrigerator magnet of Misty for The Chariot and plastic bookmarks for themselves.

The visit to Annapolis was sort of a letdown after all the memorable sights and observations of the past several weeks. But Tommy no longer waivered on his choice. Still his dream of the future was to be an Annapolis graduate. He had plenty of time to convince Chad to change his choice of West Point. But wow, the wagers of every Army and Navy game from now on would be awesome. Right now everyone was looking forward to Alaska.

It was a joyous homecoming when they finally drove into Amy's driveway in Wellesley. They had been in constant touch with Amy and Bob Holloway in Paris. Bob was returning to the States to expedite his retirement and firm up further plans to marry Amy. Would wonders never cease! The evasive, much sought after bachelor was finally snagged.

Bob was at the door to greet the vagabonds, as he had named the four of them. He had been in Paris for New Year's Eve and remained there until just a week before The Chariot's arrival. Everyone was talking at once, while Nell and Millie checked out all their secret places around the yard. Bob demanded silence, long enough to briefly describe his engagement to Amy. He had proposed to her at their favorite restaurant, L'Exchange, on the Rue Mouffetard on the Left Bank, just a short walk from the university. They had become the closest of friends as well as lovers, sharing their thoughts during their many walks along the Seine.

They had set no date for the marriage, as they wanted to wait until the vagabonds had returned from Alaska; by then, Amy would have completed her studies at the

Sorbonne. Then another home wedding, and hopefully, they could borrow The Chariot for their honeymoon to parts unknown. Hearing those plans left everyone in a real upbeat mood. Just think, they would be close to being one big family. That would prove to be much closer than anyone, except Bob and Amy, were aware of at the moment.

That night after Cass and the boys had retired, Lane and Bob stayed up very late with "man talk," or so Cass thought. But it was much, much more than that.

As requested by Amy, Bob had opened her private safe to read the final and decisive results into the investigation of Archer's life. They both agreed that Lane should describe the contents of those pages with Cass alone. Lane knew that she would need his strong and protective arms around her when the explosive truth was divulged. Lane would know when the time was right.

Everyone slept late the next morning. Lane had barely closed his eyes due to his pondering over how to discuss this totally unexpected news with Cass. He heard the boys out in the kitchen area sharing some of their experiences with Bob. As soon as Cass stirred, Lane enfolded her in his arms and waited for her to fully awaken.

"Madam Queen, are you wide awake? I have something that we must discuss in private, even before breakfast. Be my sweetheart and throw some cold water on your face while I get you a cup of coffee."

Bewildered, Cass threw on her robe while heading toward the bathroom.

"Not even time for a shower? Can't wait, so hurry, huh? Is it good news or bad news?"

Lane quickly escaped to the kitchen, pretending not to hear her last question. He greeted Bob and the boys and suggested they go ahead with their breakfast and whatever other plans they had for the day, like cleaning out The Chariot, airing their sleeping bags, and exercising Nell and Millie, anything to keep them busy. Bob understood and assured Lane that he would supervise their activities, even do the breakfast dishes.

33

Silently and more than just a bit apprehensive, Cass sat awaiting Lane's return. What could be so secret a problem that he must discuss it privately? Had their plans changed? Why? It certainly had to do with Bob and Lane's late night conversation behind closed doors in the den. She had been too tired last night to wonder about that and had fallen into a sound sleep as soon as her head hit the pillow. She had not heard Lane come to bed so had no idea that their conference lasted until nearly daylight.

Lane finally returned with steaming coffee, two cups and some Danish.

"Cass, I cannot beat around the bush about this. It is too important, so here it is, flat out, and as gently as I can present it. Amy had left instructions in her safe for Bob to follow when we all returned here."

"My God, is there something wrong with Amy? What, Lane, what?" By now Cass's hands holding her coffee were trembling violently.

"No, Cass, it was the final report on your Archer."

Slowly and precisely, Cass placed her cup on the end table and looked Lane directly in the eyes.

"This is the bad news then, or is it good news?" Lane wrapped his arms about her.

"Cass," in close to a whisper, "your Archer did not survive a plane crash but did leave a son—your grandson, Chad Fielding."

Cass did not collapse. She was numbed by such a shocking disclosure. She felt as though her seams were splitting with all the sawdust leaking out.

"Please say that again, slowly, Lane. I'm not certain that I understand."

Lane softly repeated his news, word for word, with a gigantic lump in his throat, while watching Cass speechlessly quaking, not a sound of sobs, but with rainbow droplets of tears flowing.

"Take a deep breath, Cass, and either you can ask questions or I will try to pull this together for you."

"Who was he, Lane? Where did he live? Who adopted him? What was his name? Oh, dear God, you just said Chad is his son, Chad Fielding. And Amy is a Fielding. What is the connection, Lane? Then Chad is Amy's grandson by marriage. But I am his biological grandmother. Are they certain of that? Do they have proof? How long has Amy known this? Was there a note to me from Amy? Does Chad know about this? How long has Archer been dead? Oh, my God, that was the plane crash from which you rescued Chad! What shall I do? Is he legally mine or Amy's or whose? He has no other family now, Lane. Didn't you explain that his mother did not survive the plane crash either and that his grandparents had also passed on?

"I cannot understand how Amy kept this information from me for so long and why. Was she afraid that I would try to take Chad from her? Lane, after all these years I have a family. Thank God, you are here. I'm not sure that I could handle this all alone. What shall I do? What were Bob's feelings? When shall we tell Chad, and how will be feel about my giving up my baby, his father, for adoption? Is he old enough to understand that? Let's adopt them both, Chad and Tommy. We did discuss that earlier, didn't we, however briefly." Cass was pacing the floor now, still trembling, her coffee cold, and completely forgotten.

"Now, sweetheart, take a few deep breaths, a long hot shower, get dressed, and I will answer all your questions.

Bob and the boys are cleaning out The Chariot and then are going to McDonald's, so we have plenty of time to decide what to do. And yes, there is one definite affirmation—I do want to adopt both boys. We can set those plans into action before we leave for Alaska. Then all the paperwork and court proceedings can grind along while we are away. Amy knew how badly you would want Chad and has agreed to help in any way possible to speed along the adoption process, okay? Now, try to calm down, and let's have our breakfast. I do love you so much, but I'm starved. Everything is going to be just fine, I'm sure of it."

All during the refreshing shower, Cass repeated, as if a mantra, "My Archer. My Archer. My Archer. But oh, my God, my Archer is dead! And his name wasn't Archer. Hadn't Chad said that his father's name was Todd Fielding, and Amy had told her that Chad's grandfather was Arnold Fielding, her ex-husband? Yes, that was it. She remembered now. If she could adopt Chad, would he want to keep his name, Fielding? or would he accept Hamilton? Tommy would want Hamilton, she knew that. But those decisions could be made at the proper time.

When Bob Holloway and the boys burst into the kitchen, Chad was bubbling.

"Cass, did you know that Bob once set a baby giraffe's broken leg? Great, huh? Isn't he something else? Did you ever do anything like that, Lane? You're awful quiet, Cass, are you okay?"

Cass's eyes had followed every gesture of Chad's, knowing now that her very blood coursed through his veins. He was her very own grandchild. Before shimmering tears started to overflow, Lane grabbed everyone's attention.

"I've never mended a baby animal's leg, but right now I'm in the process of trying to mend a broken heart. And that I can do with lots of help from you, Chad."

"Help mend a broken heart? Me? Whose? It can't be any of us. Amy is okay, isn't she? What can I do?"

Bob sat with his elbow on the table, his hand supporting his chin. Tommy was speechless and, for some reason, feeling very wary. Cass did not move. She wanted to wrap her arms around Chad and hold him tightly to her, but right now, she needed Lane's comforting arm about her shoulder.

"Well, Chad, this is very serious business. I certainly don't want to put a damper on our excitement of the past few weeks, but we must discuss this right now."

"Should I leave?" Tommy whispered. "Should I go outside with Nell and Millie? It sounds like family stuff to me, and I don't think I belong here right now."

"Absolutely not, Tommy, you are involved in this, too. First of all, Chad, you have already told us of your knowledge that your dad was adopted and that his name was Todd Fielding, right? Your adoptive grandfather, Arnold Fielding, whom you have also lost, was Amy's husband at one time, right?"

"Yup, you're right. That's why Amy is my grandmother. But now I've got two grannies, right Cass?"

"You are absolutely right, precious Chad," biting her lower lip, Cass went on. "In fact, I am your biological grannie. I am Todd's mother." Cass did not move toward Chad, not knowing what his reaction would be. Biological probably meant nothing to a ten-year-old boy.

"I don't know what biological means, but as long as you are my Cass, it doesn't make any difference." Slightly frowning, he added, "But if you were dad's mother, where have you been all my life? How come my name is Fielding? And who is Archer that I have heard you and Lane talking about?"

Again, Lane saved the day.

"That, we will explain to you very soon, but it's only

one half of what we hope is good news. How would you and Tommy like to be brothers? Cass and I want to legally adopt both of you."

Dead silence! Now, even Bob Holloway's eyes were brimming with tears. His glance roamed back and forth from Chad to Tommy.

"How can a couple of guys get so lucky?"

Tommy's eyes were as large as basketballs his mouth agape, hardly breathing.

"Are you s-saying that Ch-Chad and I would really b-be brothers?" he stuttered, totally choked up. "That I w-will never have to g-go back to the orphanage? That my n-name would be T-Tommy Hamilton? That you would b-be my mother and f-father or something?" He leaped into Lane's lap. "Awesome."

Chad was still puzzled, but he wrapped his arms about Cass's neck.

"I never want to lose you, Cass!" he sobbed. "I love you so much. I don't want to be anywhere except with you, Lane, and Tommy, ever!"

"You never will, Chad, my long-lost love. I have searched for your father for many, many years, only to find that he has gone from us, but that he has left you to heal my broken heart." Emotions were heavy on everyone's part.

"Now, guys, why don't you give each other a high-five, continue with your work on The Chariot, and start getting used to being brothers, huh? As of today, Bob, Cass, and I will get the ball rolling on the adoption papers. We'll let that process work out while we are in Alaska. Then when we return, we really will be one big family, including Amy and Bob."

34

Chad and Tommy were not at all concerned with the intricacies of adoption. They knew that if Lane said that they would be brothers, they would be. All that was on their mind presently was that they would never be separated again, at least until they went to college. While Bob kept them busy rearranging The Chariot, Lane had one more bombshell to drop on Cass. Amy had left a sealed letter for her.

My dear Cass,
    It had to be a miracle that you chose me to try to help you in your dilemma of so many months ago. It surely must have been destiny that we were to become such close friends. This whole experience tends to prove that truth is much stranger than fiction. You well know that I dearly love Chad but cannot and will not deprive him of his rightful legacy. I am so thankful that he will be legally yours and am deeply grateful that he will be given a wholesome set of values by you and Lane. He is a very lucky boy and loves you dearly as well as needs you badly.
    It is my sincere hope that you will forgive me for withholding the information derived from my search for your son. You were an extremely troubled and guilt-ridden lady when you first became my client. When you met Lane and found that you were no longer cynical about men and bitter about life in general, I so much wanted you to find happiness in your life, which you certainly deserve. Your relationship with Lane and Chad has expanded to depths far beyond my highest hopes. We all, including Bob, love you deeply and want nothing but your happiness and security.

Now that your life has turned completely around and that your faith in people has returned, I have but one request. Having read your manuscript, "The Clay Pigeon," it is my hope that you will continue. There are many, many "pigeons" out there who cannot help but benefit from your experience. There is so much that you can still include that will help other "marks" in their struggle of being a single woman. In my office, within your personal file, I have left suggestions for you to use if you wish.

In my practice, I have tried to help many women with their troubled lives. You are one who has made it through the maze successfully and are in a position to help others. Please take the files with you on your trip to Alaska, along with your incomplete manuscript. Don't make a chore of continuing to write, but do try to weave it into your busy life. I will always be available to assist in any way and have all the faith in the world that you will be highly successful in this venture. You have had the first-hand experience as well as the educational background to get your helpful words into print. Please do it, Cass! I send this with all my love and faith in you.

Amy

Having finished the letter, Cass, scarcely breathing, stared off into space. Quietly, but closely observing her reaction to the letter, Lane refrained from speaking for some minutes.

"Amy is such a good friend, Lane, I would like to share her letter with you."

Lane smiled and nodded in the affirmative. When he finished, he sighed and asked Cass what she thought about Amy's request.

"It seems so long ago, Lane. Now, it is almost as though all those characters in the manuscript are total strangers, including Sue and me. You have read my work so far, what do you think? Should I leave the past in the past or develop the writing into something that hopefully would be of help to others?"

"Cass, my love, I don't want your life to be cluttered with anything that you don't want to do. There is no reason to make a decision right now. Let's take the material with us to Alaska, and if you feel that you want to continue, do it. There is no reason for it to disrupt our enjoyment of traveling. If you choose to go ahead with the project, you can always wait until we return, right?"

"You are always so sensible, Lane. Of course, you are right. Let's just pack away all the material, and I'll make the decision later."

It was a busy time as all preparations for Alaska proceeded smoothly. Together, Bob and Lane contacted all concerned regarding the adoption of Chad and Tommy. Their past professional involvement with so many people of influence helped tremendously to expedite matters.

Each night, they called Amy to keep her up to date on their progress and decisions. She missed her friends but knew that a full and unquestionably exciting and contented future lay ahead. In the past, she had been secretly concerned about properly bringing up Chad alone, by herself. But now, all those worries had been miraculously solved for her. Bob assured her that he would return to Paris as soon as the Hamiltons were on their way. Amy had a warm and fuzzy feeling each time Bob referred to Lane, Chad, Cass, and Tommy as the Hamiltons. Could any puzzle ever have been so blissfully solved? She doubted it.

Cass was on cloud nine during all preparations. She thanked the Good Lord each night in her prayers, being certain in her mind that a higher power surely had been woven into all the positive answers to her hopes and dreams.

Most ten-year-old boys pictured Alaska as the frozen North, all ice and snow year-round, Eskimos with fur-lined parkas living in igloos, with freely roaming polar bears, walruses, and sea lions everywhere. But Chad and Tommy knew better, as Cass had included the forty-ninth state in their social studies curriculum. They would remember that Juneau is the capital, Anchorage the largest city, forget-me-nots the state flower, and willow ptarmigan the state bird, as well as Mount McKinley the highest point. That was also one of the highest points in their anticipation, as Lane had assured everyone that they would be camping at the base of Mount McKinley.

Everyone had studied road maps and were amazed that so little of that huge state could be reached by highway. That problem was solved by so many owning their own planes. It seemed uncanny to the boys that when children had birthday parties, their dads would pick up their friends in their own private plane, then return them after the party. "Awesome! That does it, Chad, we must plan to get a pilot's license some day."

35

All arrangements were secure, with the same caretaker at Amy's home for the summer. The Hamiltons dropped Bob Holloway at Logan Airport in Boston for his flight back to Paris, then headed north toward Montreal and the Trans-Canada Highway. Chad and Tommy closely followed the maple leaf markers on the map for the Trans-Canada while keeping notes of new sights and mileage each day. They were curious about the Sudbury, Ontario, area, which appeared to be an extremely barren rock fault for miles in all directions. That same day, they passed through Indian country, truly an Indian village. Tommy's comment was, "Ten to one the proverbial wild Indian is no wilder than some of my friends back at the orphanage." His sense of humor was a delight to all.

Cass had commented on what great condition the Trans-Canada Highway was kept. With a sly wink and grin, Lane followed up with, "That figures, they've only got one." It was surprising that the highway was only two lanes and nearly all patrolled by aircraft. So far, there had been many, many Provincial Park campsites with sand boxes, showers, Laundromats, and fireplaces with plenty of wood, all very clean and constantly patrolled. They were impressed with the great number of first-aid stations, as well as lots of ice.

Before the first week was out, Chad and Tommy had conspired to make use of their cordless microphones.

"Let's read ahead in our AAA tour books and take turns being travel guides. Will you be first, Chad, tomorrow morning?"

"Good morning, friends." Totally surprised, Lane and

Cass were jolted in their seats, then broke into spasms of laughter. Nell and Millie looked about for the strange voice, but quieted down promptly. Chad continued very slowly and distinctly, "I am your tour guide for the day and hope to answer any questions that you may have. There has been some curiosity regarding the barren expanse back in Sudbury, Ontario. I can now inform you that that was an area of extensive nickel and copper mines.

"Just ahead, we will be shopping in Sault Sainte Marie, and please notice the free youth hostel, which will be one huge tent at the entrance to the city. The stay is limited to twenty-four hours only. From Sault Sainte Marie to WaWa, we will be traveling on the east shore at the very water's edge of Lake Superior, which will be very rocky with surf pounding and sending up spray. Also, please note the many birch and tamarack trees as well as sea gulls. For those of you who are looking for wild life, keep a sharp lookout for moose. I have been told that Bull Winkle is vacationing in the area.

"For the gem enthusiasts aboard, there is a tremendous amount of amethyst in western Ontario. We will be seeing many little, withered old men, some of them Indians, who have set up their tables in front of their shanty palaces to beckon the tourists—sort of an invitation to come and see and hopefully purchase some of their jewels. By all appearances, we will be filling the tank again in Thunder Bay. You will find it interesting that from nearby Raith, Ontario, all rivers flow north to the Arctic Ocean. Tomorrow we will be entering Lake of the Woods tourist region and crossing the border into Manitoba. I do sincerely hope that you have enjoyed my chat about the province of Ontario!" To Chad the applause was deafening. Lane, Cass, and Tommy had truly enjoyed the presentation of his research.

"Good morning, fellow travelers, this is Tommy H. Hamilton. The H stands for hopefully." Cass and Lane nodded enthusiastically and reached across the aisle to shake hands on that comment. "We are now entering the province of Manitoba and are approximately seventeen hundred and fifty miles from our driveway in Wellesley, Massachusetts. Please note the pride in the cleanliness of the Canadian people. How can we miss the many signs that remind us to 'Put Your Trash Into Orbit', the orbit being a capsule-type sphere marked Orbit every few miles.

"Our first stop will be White Shell Beach, where I'm sure we'll remain more than overnight. It will be a great place for Nell and Millie, as well as a chance for all of us swim. Our driver needs a day or two to relax. Then we will progress to Winnepeg, where, I might add, Gerry and Ray's Steak House is highly recommended, in case the cook also needs a break. Beyond Winnepeg, the capital of Manitoba, we will be off again into prairie country—flat, wide open spaces for miles in all directions, acres and acres of wheat fields, and huge herds of short horns (beef cattle). Our driver will note that driving will be a little more difficult, as the wind really whips across these highways.

"We are heading north to Riding Mountain National Park, where we will join the buffalo herds. We can expect to find at least two herds with approximately twenty-five to thirty animals in each herd. Warning signs forbid pedestrians, bicycles, and motorcycles as well as 'Do not leave your car' reminders. Buffalos have poor eye sight but can run up to thirty-five miles an hour and are also excellent swimmers. The bulls weigh about twenty-four hundred pounds and are very protective of the rest of their herd. Upon leaving Riding Mountain National Park we must return to the highway, then on to Regina, Saskatchewan. We have traveled over two thousand miles to date. Enjoy, and I will be returning with further hints for the traveler in a day or two."

36

"Before crossing into the next province, what kind of a fee are you guys charging for your educational travelogue? You two are real foxes, aren't they, Cass?"

"You can be certain of that, Lane. Have you noticed that they are also taping their comments? They will have enough material for English themes all the way through college."

"Right, Cass," chimed in Chad, "and have you noticed that these poor Canadian kids are still in school?"

"Bet they'd rather have Cass as a tutor and be traveling in The Chariot, huh, Chad?" Tommy still felt that all this was a dream. "And besides, we've gotta' earn our keep somehow, because taking care of Nell and Millie certainly aren't chores. They're our buddies."

"You got that right, Tommy. Now, I'd better get ready for tomorrow to introduce you to another new province. Only three more to go, then *Alaska*. Wow!"

Chad and Tommy had whispered for many hours into the night about their legally becoming brothers. One of their discussions brought tears to their eyes.

"Gee, Chad, you know that your name would be Chad Fielding Hamilton. I don't know what my name was. When I was found in a basket on the steps of the orphanage, no one else knew either, so they named me for a street nearby, Falcon Street. So I'd be Thomas Falcon Hamilton. Hey, and y'know what? We'd have the same middle and last initials, right? If only they had named me Charlie, our monograms would be exactly alike. Wow! But let's face it; at least that street that they named me for wasn't turkey. You'd never let me live that down. They picked the right bird that time, huh?"

It was Chad's turn to introduce the next province, and he was anxious and ready.

"Good morning, everyone. This is Chad Fielding Hamilton, I hope, your guide through the province of Saskatchewan." He wondered why Lane and Cass reached out to each other to join hands and smile. Lane winked in the rearview mirror and nodded his head approvingly. Chad had no way of knowing how many hours they had spent wondering whether he would choose to keep Fielding or become Hamilton when the time came to sign the legal adoption papers.

"I'm sure you have noticed the hundreds of oil wells throughout southern Manitoba. And across this province not only oil and natural gas, but there are many acres of wheat, rye, oats, and barley—also some flax, potash, and salt. To the right of this highway, we will be paralleling the Canadian Pacific Railroad, which ships cars from Detroit across the prairies. Yup, there they are, flat cars loaded with what appears to be General Motors and Ford vehicles.

"We are now approaching Regina, the capital city of Saskatchewan and also the largest. The provincial flower is the prairie lily, and we can certainly see why. Have you noticed that the majority of houses that we can see from the parkway are stucco? There is very little timber on the prairie. Most homes huddle together with just a walkway between them, while just outside of town, it is an unbroken expanse of land.

"Our next overnight stop will be Moose Jaw at the Prairie Oasis Campground. That's an interesting name as we all know of oases in the desert, but it's a first to find one on the prairie, right? We are presently about twenty miles east of Moose Jaw, and there is a sign for the town of Drinkwater. My other family knew a naval officer named Drinkwater once. I wonder what happened to him. But as Tommy just told me, 'Don't digress'! He must have been studying his vocabulary, huh Cass? But then, he can study pretty late at night these days, 'cause it's never dark until ten or ten-thirty.

"Tomorrow I can almost guarantee that you will see plenty of tumbleweed, because the weather forecast is rain and high winds. It is high time that we spot some prairie dogs, too. Keep a close watch! Perhaps our friendly Canadian Mounties will tell us more about the salt flats in Val Jean. I do know that the extensive fields of brilliant yellow blooms are mustard. Lots of cactus are appearing now, too, and you will see that their blossoms look like begonias, yellow and peach.

"I do hope that everyone is aware of the fact that July fourth is fast approaching, today being the first. Hopefully, we can spend at least three days in the national parks as we approach the Rockies. And did anyone have their radio on late last night? The Canadians are getting ready to celebrate our Independence Day, too. I did hear an impressive tribute to America out of Nashville, Tennessee, even though Canada just passed a law that all music on the Canadian Broadcasting System must be thirty percent Canadian. That sounds fair, right?

"I will sign off here in Saskatchewan and look forward to crossing to the next province. Meanwhile perhaps our driver will try out the CB for awhile. Maybe someone will have their ears on. Shall we try, Lane? Let's see, it's been a while. You are Medic, Cass is Voo Doo Chile, Tommy is Commodore, and I'm still Pointer. Sorry that we haven't found more wild life for you, Tommy, but better days are coming, or do you suppose you'll have to wait for some wild life at Annapolis?"

37

"Today we will pass through Medicine Hat and Calgary in the province of Alberta. We will be by-passing, to our north, the capital city of Edmonton, but possibly will visit there on the return trip. Please, don't anyone doze off as on our approach to Banff National Park, we will be treated to our first sight of the famed Rocky Mountains. There are no adjectives in my vocabulary to describe the beauty of the Jasper-Banff Highway, just that it is indescribably beautiful. The lakes are all turquoise in color and surrounded by glaciers, especially Lake Louise, where we will be spending our Fourth of July, still in the province of Alberta.

"In all the many campsites, there are warning signs everywhere, 'Do not feed or attempt to approach a bear'. The Mounties will explain that the bears' survival instinct urges them to approach food, and they sense that they are protected in the parks. Troublesome or known vicious animals are taken back into the wild country or disposed of for the protection of all. All trash cans in picnic areas and campsites are hanging by chains from high metal T-bars to prevent wild life from foraging. We are all anxious now to get to Alaska so have decided to omit the ski mobile rides on the Columbia ice fields. Hard to believe, during the month of July, but watch for the ice buses, too. All this area is constantly patrolled by the Royal Canadian Mounted Police in helicopters.

"Tomorrow we will leave Jasper National Park and cross into British Columbia, mountain goat country. We will be leaving the turquoise lakes and rivers for a darker green, as opposed to the deep blue of New England. Did

I mention that we left the Trans-Canada Highway back at Lake Louise in Alberta? You will be very much aware of this from Mount Robson National Park, northward. There will be two-lane roads with no barrier between the highway and the more than one-thousand-foot drop. No stepping out of The Chariot, or we drop out of sight.

"On to Prince George, Hazelton, and Terrace along the Skeena River to Prince Rupert, the halibut capital of the world, and finally the ferry terminal for the Alaskan Marine Highway. The Skeena River is low in the valley with mountains rising abruptly on both sides. The Canadian Pacific Railroad will be within six feet on our right with the river the same distance on our left. In places, the glacier had dropped to ground level and had to be cut away for trains to pass.

"From here on, we will be informing you of only the high points of the inland passage of the Alaskan Marine Highway, such as Ketchikan, Wrangell, St. Petersburg, Juneau, the state capital, Skagway, and Haines, where we will dock. Then we must pass through customs at the entrance to the Yukon Territories. Enjoy your ferry trip, everyone."

The Chariot was in line with other standbys at 4:45 A.M. for boarding the ship. Their stateroom was available, but regulations stated that Millie and Nell must be kept in the vehicle. That was no problem, because the boys elected to sleep in the motor home rather than the stateroom, then they could whisper long into the night and bother no one. Lane had checked the schedule for mail stops so that the dogs could be taken ashore briefly. That was fun, too, even in the middle of the night. Everyone aboard was enthralled with the myna bird traveling in one of the cabins. It talked continuously and mimicked every sound from a laugh, sneeze, cough, or conversation. Also on board in a nearby motor home from Michigan was a pet fox, a hound dog, and a racoon, plus three kids.

The boys were on deck when the ship entered Glacier Bay at 5:00 A.M. It sailed through waters as smooth as a mirror, reflecting the clear blue sky as they moved deeper into the bay past older growth of hemlock and spruce to newer growth of alders. Park officers who had come aboard at Bartlett Cove explained everything and helped to spot whales, mountain goats, bald eagles, and black bears. They were also treated to a sea otter's dream, spotting wrinkled, whiskered faces looking up as they passed. Some floated on their backs, munching contentedly on mussels and clams. Others dove and splashed or simply bobbed in the icy waters.

Later in the day, they were seen forming "rafts" by holding on to one another as they drifted, creating a sort of floating party. Although the largest raft they saw was made up of about a dozen otters, the guide pointed out that sometimes there were as many as thirty at one time. The view was spectacular, surrounded by monstrous glaciers whose walls were more than a hundred feet high. Suddenly like a cannon shot a chunk of ice the size of a building broke off and fell into the bay. Water spray and chunks of ice flew up and crashed thunderously down, resulting in huge waves that made the ship rock.

After docking and driving forty-three miles to get through customs, there was a "must visit" at the Yukon Wildlife Preserve, near Whitehorse in the Yukon Territory. The boys were busy taking pictures of grazing musk oxen, bison, and on the cliffs, Dall sheep. But they were all anxious to get back on the Alaska Highway to Fairbanks, where they would see a famous man-made wonder, The Trans-Canada pipeline, which extends eight hundred miles, from the Arctic Ocean to Valdez on the southern coast of Alaska at Prince William Sound.

Then on to the Savage River Campground at the base

of Mount McKinley, the highest peak in North America. Next was a shopping trip in Tok, Alaska, and a visit to the Alkan Kennel to see the famous Siberian and Alaskan huskies. On the tour from Mount McKinley in Denali National Park to Anchorage Lane popped another surprise.

"Are you guys anxious to head back east, or could I suggest that we hire a bush pilot to fly us to Nome for the day for a visit to an authentic Eskimo village? There are no highways to access that area, so we must fly."

Dead silence—the boys were speechless.

"But will a bush pilot take all of us, Nell and Millie, too?"

"No, Chad, Cass and I have already discussed that. The dogs cannot go, but Cass prefers to stay with The Chariot and work on one of her projects, okay? Are you game?"

"Awesome! Are you sure you'll be all right all alone, Cass? If it's a secure campground and you'll be safe, I'd love to go. But I don't want anything to happen to my new mother."

With tears in her eyes, Cass gave Tommy a big hug, assuring him that she would be perfectly safe and would truly prefer to stay in Anchorage.

"I'll save my strength, because we are going back to Tok and cross over to the Klondike Highway to Dawson City and south to the Klondike goldfields where we can pan for gold, okay? Then back to the States, or the 'lower forty-nine,' as they call us. You guys just go and enjoy it. But don't forget your cameras and the pocket-size tape recorders."

38

Cass felt slightly guilty, but she was really looking forward to a day to herself. She could call the lawyers to check on the adoption status and possibly do some work on *The Clay Pigeon* manuscript that she had started so very long ago. She had promised her dear friend and confidante, Amy, that she would try to complete the project, and she must not disappoint her.

After exercising Nell and Millie, Cass sat down to a quiet cup of tea while her thoughts roamed to Chad's father, Todd Fielding, whom she had carried in her heart as Archer for so very long. The day would come when Chad would want to know why his dad, Todd, had been adopted and why his true grandfather and Cass had not married. She wondered whether to explain now or wait until Chad asked her. He seemed so young to understand anything so convoluted. But what if he never did ask? Was it on his mind already and for some reason was afraid to ask? Was he too young to understand her dire circumstances at the time Todd was born?

Both little boys, Chad and Tommy, must wonder in the dark of the night who their biological parents and grandparents really were. At least Chad knew that Cass was his father's real mother, but Tommy had no knowledge of his birth circumstances. Just perhaps, they could trace Tommy's background and discuss their situations together as a family. For now, if Lane agreed, it might be best to let them enjoy being brothers. She had no doubt that the adoption papers of both boys would be processed successfully.

Cass's thoughts drifted back to the day when she

found that she was pregnant. Rand Mitchell was completing his third year at West Point so could not marry until he graduated. They had been together since the beginning of his schooling as a United States Army officer but had never been officially engaged. In fact, Rand had never actually even mentioned marriage, but she loved him too much to interfere with his carefully planned future. She did not want a forced marriage just because she was pregnant, nor did Rand need to proceed with his life carrying a burden of guilt. There was no way that she could support a child, so her only option had been adoption, with the hope of finding her baby some day. Would Chad understand this?

She shuddered to think that she very briefly had considered abortion. Thankfully her conscience steered her to the right choice. Rand had graduated and was promptly sent overseas; he returned in a body bag, never knowing that he had a son. Cass had kept a file on Rand Mitchell, vowing that some day she would find her son and explain the reasons why she and Rand had never married. She was certain that Chad would be proud that his biological grandfather was a West Point graduate as well as his father—and that he would follow in their footsteps as the third generation. Chad was not aware yet that sons of Medal of Honor winners were entitled by law to go to West Point. She certainly must share that knowledge with him soon. Enough of that line of thought for now. Lane would know what to do.

Cass unpacked her notes on *The Clay Pigeon*. She must try to offer in print some advice to other desolated women, the clay pigeons of society whose possible downfall was the men in their lives. Let them know that they must believe in themselves first, not depend on others for their peace of mind and happiness. At least she could offer some pitfalls that they might avoid. She could begin by trying to convince others that love and sex were not the same. A fair warning was that sex just might be a desire not to be lonely, a search to find an intimate human connection.

One must try to understand that for men, love is a very powerful impulse, immensely sexual in character, all desire and speed and yet quickly over with. Afterwards, his thoughts are drawn to other matters and his partner feels forsaken. For a woman, love constitutes the whole of life, while the man takes an interest in his attainment for success in his work. If women have an understanding of this, it might alleviate the loss of that sense of worth, so she must keep a life and interests of her own. It does help to keep reminding oneself that true love is based on faith, trust, respect, understanding, and a deep commitment to one other person.

It is understandingly difficult when one is lonely to avoid the womanizer's appeal and to slither away intact even when one knows that she is playing with fire. Rest assured that the Don Juan types fear long-term intimacy and so avoid permanent relationships. Despite his charisma, watch for his need for constant admiration. He is not so much interested in the woman herself, but in the way she responds to him. The true object of his admiration is *himself,* not women. Be on alert for this narcissism. He must have repeated proof of his attractiveness by trying to conquer woman after woman. Even though you tell him over and over how great he is, he starts to wonder if other women would agree.

He will look for a woman's fatal flaw and invest in it, play on her vulnerability and hopes. Be careful not to contribute to your own downfall by helping to advance a romance with such an exploiter. Don't be blind to the lack of depth in such a man. If you know that the relationship is not going to work, look at the man as a charming scoundrel, very alive and fun to be with, but just not possible as a lifetime mate. If you can manage this and still enjoy his company, you can come out of the affair unscathed.

As Amy had tried to explain to Cass in her therapy sessions, we must try to understand each other in the search for a true and lasting relationship. And to really understand is to listen without criticism and judgment. We must not have secrets from one another, even though we sometimes will not share our thoughts or actions in order to avoid arguments.

Another offered warning seemed to be that boredom is the greatest of all enemies to a committed relationship. The day should never come when partners no longer have anything to discover or to say to each other. It is important to know that such thoughts as sharing childhood memories, emotionally charged incidents in one's life, not only pain inflicted by others, but the beautiful memories, will bring much more integration to a partnership.

Cass reviewed some more of the advice and warnings from her therapy sessions. *Beware* seemed one that should be emphasized, *Beware*, which essentially means *be aware*. Don't see another person as you think he is; let him gradually reveal what he really is. And be very careful about giving another person power over you, as they will often misuse it. Watch out for the passive-aggressive types, losers, who get what they want by making you feel sorry for them.

On the plus side when considering a man, ask not about his age, but his reliability, his kindness, his sense of honor, his honesty, his sense of humor, his ability to think in an emergency, and the way he takes care of others. And pertaining to all of us, we must remember that having character is evidenced in our actions, in the values by which we live. Honesty, discipline, reverence, industriousness, compassion, forgiveness, devotion, courage, kindness, grace, and gratitude are among the qualities that integrity of character produce.

"*Good grief!*" exploded Cass to the degree that Nell and Millie raised their heads with ears twitching, "I am trying to expound like a psychologist or a psychiatrist or a psychotherapist, which I certainly am not qualified to do. Would Amy understand that delving into her manuscript was dredging up unpleasant memories? It was bound to effect her emotions in the future. Her life now was Lane, Chad, and Tommy. In all fairness to them, she would send all this material to Sue, whose life paralleled Cass's and who was perfectly capable of finishing the manuscript. Amy would agree with this decision, of that she was certain." Cass repackaged the material with a very definite stamp of finality.

39

Now that Cass had made the difficult decision to pass on the completion of "The Clay Pigeon" to Sue, she could relax. Rather than lounging in a sun chair outside, she opted to snack on last night's left-over pizza, close the curtains and pamper herself with a cozy nap. There would be plenty of time to prepare dinner before Lane and the boys returned, and Nell and Millie had been exercised, so were content to stretch out on their beds in front of the entrance.

She fell into such a deep sleep that she was not aware that the door, which she surely thought she had locked, was slowly opening. The muffled whimpers from the dogs went unheeded. Why was she having trouble breathing? Cass clawed at her mouth to find it totally sealed with, oh, my God, some kind of tape. Why? Who were these masked terrorists who were trashing The Chariot? Where were Nell and Millie, and why were they so quiet? She raised up to a sitting position in abject terror. The dogs were prone with muzzles and legs taped.

Amid all this horrifying invasion, her first thought was not what the invaders were searching for, but how much it would hurt to remove the tape from Nell and Millie's thick hair. The strangers were ignoring her completely. Why didn't they ask her where the traveler's checks, credit cards, and other valuables were hidden? Even if they were professionals, they would never find the ignition keys. Lane was too clever for that, and even if they tried to force the information, they would have to go to the office for them. She would say that Lane had taken them with him—a weak excuse but that was all she could think of presently.

Perhaps they weren't interested in taking the vehicle, knowing that it would be almost impossible to get by the park security guards in order to leave. Now they were raiding the refrigerator and throwing the food into a plastic trash bag. Poor Nell and Millie were noiselessly thrashing about on the carpeting. Everything from the cupboards and closets was strewn about, but, thankfully, they had left the dogs room to breathe. Could she describe these raiders? She must concentrate on that.

Why leather, brass-studded jackets with lots of zippers in this weather? Hoods covered their heads, but they must be either fairly young or in good physical condition, as neither was out of breath from the exertion of all their frantic efforts. Their boots were the pointed, steel-toed cowboy types and well worn. Bikers? Slowly one approached her to put his arm about her shoulder. Oh, my God, not that! Cass shuddered and felt the nausea rising in her throat as she became dizzy and faint. How could they know her name, calling her, "Cass! Cass!"

"Cass, wake up! Wake up! Why are you sobbing, another one of your nightmares?" It was Lane sitting beside her on the edge of the bed with his protective arms about her.

The boys were terrified, their mouths agape and eyes brimming with tears. What would make their Cass cry? They loved her too much to see her like this. Maybe they should never have left her alone. Nell and Millie sensed the tension as their muzzles prodded Cass's tightly-clenched fists. She was drenched with perspiration. She slowly came to realize that it all had been an alarming dream.

"Okay, guys, no harm done, just a bad dream. No

more cold pizza for me, ever. Next time I will at least heat it! Let's go outside in the sunshine while you tell me all about your flight and show me all your souvenirs. Did you find the walrus tusk carvings? Then we'll prepare dinner. You must be starving, right?"

It was a joyful reunion with everybody chattering, opening gifts and lighting the grille. When things quieted down, Chad remembered the mail that they had picked up at the office.

"Lane, what was that yellow envelope that you opened and were grinning from ear to ear all about?"

"Yup, right. Now's the time. I was saving the best till last." Slowly drawing the telegram from his inside jacket pocket, he clasped Cass's hand and breathlessly read, "'Congratulations to all the Hamiltons! Adoption papers cleared! Come home for the signatures and celebration. All our love, Amy and Bob.'"

With long, teary-eyed sighs and lots of hugs, they quickly finished the salad and grilled hamburgers.

"Gosh, are we going straight home now?" Tommy whispered, all choked up.

"Let's study our maps, okay? As long as we're here, we can't miss seeing the redwoods in California, can we? Then we can push on to Yosemite and then, home. How does that sound? Bob has also sent a long letter, which we will read together as soon as we are geared for our trip tomorrow."

Bob's letter was jam-packed with more good news and a welcome proposal. He and Amy wanted their wedding in Wellesley, and his sense of humor glowed as he suggested that it would take little planning due to the Hamiltons being sort of a practice run. He was such a crazy and fun-loving guy. He seriously suggested that they swap homes. Cass's cozy ranch would be sufficient for Amy and him. Only two of them, whereas the Hamilton family was now six, two adults, two active sons, and their Nell and Millie. Was this a sensible idea or what! The cruise back to the East Coast now seemed almost a must-do-soon situation. They had so many plans to make—settling in their new home, registering for school in September, planning a wedding, and gearing The Cariot for a honeymoon. They all agreed that this was life as it should be.

40

Again traveling north in Alaska and back into the Yukon Territory eased their anxiety to get back to New England. The sunsets were extraordinary. The sun seemed to pop along the horizon like the little white ball in a sing-along with Mitch Miller, there to drop behind the trees. It was never completely dark. "That is because the northern hemisphere is tilted toward the sun in summer and the sun makes a 360-degree circle—in evidence always," as Tommy explained. "Clear as mud? Okay, it'll make a cool science project later, right, Chad?"

The boys were saddened at the border crossing back into the Yukon. A German shorthair had been taken from dope-pushers and impounded. Everything that is taken is sent back to Tok or Anchorage, with the possible chance of buying back the belongings at estimated costs. The sheriff who explained all this fascinated the boys by telling how he trained his own sled dogs. The lead and swing dogs were the smartest and trained for those positions. Others rotate positions unless a stubborn one refuses to work other than his favorite position.

Kluane Lake, the largest lake in the Yukon, was the point where Eastern and Western engineers had met when bulldozing for the Alkan Highway in 1942. They also found a unique Indian cemetery, where over each grave a four by six wooden house was erected. For miles, open-range country offered herds of wild range horses, beaver, mountain goat, wolverine, caribou, sheep, and black bear.

All agreed that "Beautiful British Columbia", as it says on their license plates, is definitely an understatement. It is truly magnificent. Here, the boys noted a new trick of the Mounties. On freeway-type highways, they just happened to be parked beside the road and always around a corner with the trunk lid up to hide the bubble.

Back through customs again at the Washington State line—back to the lower forty-nine. The scenic route through Washington and Oregon was breathtaking, but now everyone was looking forward to the "Avenue of the Giants" in the forests of California. The boys took many pictures of the famous chimney tree, drive-through tree, and drive-on-a-log. One tree had a butt of twenty-five feet, which were anywhere from 3,200 to 5,000 years old.

For future reference the boys took notes on the redwood trees:

"It is believed that they have been growing in California for forty million years or perhaps even longer. Coast redwoods grow extensively over an area of 1.69 million acres, stretching all along the northern California coast. The redwood region is a broken strip of irregular width but rarely reaching more than thirty miles inland.

"On the other hand, myrtlewood is found only in a small area along the Pacific coast. The dried leaves of this tree are used as a food seasoning as bay leaves. This wood has no equal for durability and historical value. It is used almost exclusively in the manufacture of fine gifts, custom gun stocks, and custom-made furniture. The United States Navy also used myrtlewood as keelblocks in its drydocks. Due to its great strength and density, the large green blocks tend to stay on the bottom when the drydock is filled with water and are quite often reused."

Cass commented that "majestic" comes into its finest descriptive purpose when referring to these gifts of nature. The whole area is the "Humboldt," as natives call it, named for the county.

Now The Chariot headed back East, via the northern

route through wheat fields, open cattle ranges, and fantastically extensive acreage of contour plowing that stretched for miles.

Much later in life, Chad and Tommy would reflect on the many, many learning experiences of their travels. Not only were they steeped in the folklore, the geographical wonders, and the history of their country, but the courtesies and avoidable pitfalls of traveling in strange territories.

One lesson that Lane had taught them was shocking, scary, and impressive to their young and naive minds. It was difficult to accept that not all people could be trusted and that they must always be aware of this for their own protection. The one experience that gave them much food for thought in this puzzling dilemma was by the roadside in the dark of night.

Anxious now to get home, the family had been traveling for many more hours than usual. Their standard travel plans were to be off the highway by dark, but this night was an exception. The dogs were restless. It was time to briefly stop where they could be walked a bit. A deserted, no-facilities rest stop was just the place. Quickly, Cass and the boys leashed Nell and Millie, hopped out, and headed for the grassy area. The dogs knew why they were out, so the stop was very, very brief.

Just as they had returned and locked the door, a pickup truck skidded up beside them and the driver yelled, "Could I have some water for my dog?" Lane promptly put The Chariot in gear and raced out of the area, with tires spitting a shower of gravel, at the greatest possible speed. The boys and Cass were thrown off balance and wide-eyed with surprise.

"Why couldn't we give him some water for his dog?" Chad questioned.

"Boys, not more than five minutes ago, we passed

through a town with at least two filling stations and a restaurant. Why didn't that stranger stop there? It is possible that he spotted our rig, saw the Massachusetts license plate, and might have figured us as a mark for robbery. That we don't need. This is one reminder to you that you must learn to *be aware* at all times. Agreed?"

"Awesome." whispered Tommy. "That's a lesson we'll never forget, right, Chad?"

"Never would have thought of it," was Chad's breathless comment.

41

A fun stop for shopping in Wyoming resulted in everyone talking Lane into buying a cowboy hat. As Lane paid the cashier, Cass and the boys returned to The Chariot to store away their purchases. They were interrupted by frantic barking intercepted by questioning glances at the door. Having been in the habit of keeping the door locked at all times, Cass peered out the window.

"Guys, come and see this! Lane is wearing his black, ten-gallon Stetson and the dogs do not recognize him." With gales of laughter, Cass called, "Please remove your hat and give the password."

Their entrance to Yellowstone National Park was sort of disappointing, as the gatekeeper announced that there were no campsites left. Their nearest campground would be a few miles back in Jackson Hole. "Wow, that's okay, that's the famous lawyer Gerry Spence's hometown!" offered Lane. It was a small campground with the first sign that they had seen warning all visitors, "Keep your pets on nothing more than a six-foot lead. This is bear country."

Back to Yellowstone early in the morning to finally see Old Faithful, which was expected to erupt approximately each hour. This is where there were grizzlies everywhere wandering leisurely about. The radio constantly warned that the grizzlies appeared fat, lazy, and placid but are truly dangerous and unpredictable.

Leaving Yellowstone, they experienced a rugged drive through the Bighorn Mountains with excellent roads but constant hairpin turns. As Lane commented, "It seems as though the steering wheel is turning more than the vehicle's wheels."

Highway 90 through South Dakota was a fast one, but they did not miss the Badlands and Mount Rushmore. It was completely shocking to see how immense the presidential carvings were. The faces alone were sixty feet, and if the whole body had been carved, they would have reached four hundred sixty-plus feet. Lincoln's nose is eighteen feet, larger than that of the Great Sphinx, according to Chief Black Elk, who gave the lectures. "An impressive old buck, huh, Chad?" whispered Tommy.

Crossing the rest of the plains in South Dakota seemed endless, and there was no list of "things to see" in Iowa. The high interest now was to head back home. Cass was surprised that chickenburgers seemed to be popular on all menus. Also, no one had ever heard of westerns, or Denvers, as Canadians and Alaskans called them. "Do you suppose they are really made with chicken? After all, hamburgers aren't made with ham!" offered Tommy.

After the many, many miles of traveling, once they had crossed the Mississippi River, it seemed like a short, straight shot home. It was a great chance to review some of their impressions while the ribbon of highway unraveled.

"You know what? I don't remember seeing a solitary potato in Idaho. They must bootleg them in from Aroostook county in Maine."

"Tommy, with conclusions like that, your possibility for success in life is extremely remote. The only academy you'll qualify for is Arthur Murray's," Chad snickered.

"Perish that thought, 'cause I hate to dance, my friend. Let's check some of our notes. Did you write down that Barrow, Alaska, is the northernmost town in the United States, only twelve hundred miles south of the North Pole? And that Nome is only two hundred miles from Russia? Boy, Alaska is well named as The Last Frontier."

Lane had been listening to their conversation so decided that now was the time to announce one more surprise. He had secreted one page of Bob's last letter to present to the boys at the most opportune time. Taking the folded page from his map folder, he nudged Cass with raised, questioning eyebrows. She nodded yes.

"Hey, guys, now that you are seriously organizing your notes, I have for you another good reason for doing just that." Passing the sheet to Chad and Tommy, he added, "I was saving this message from Bob and Amy to you, and now you need to know its contents."

The note read: "Chad and Tommy, welcome to the Hamilton family. Our celebration gift to you is a fully-equipped computer lab all set up in the den back here in Wellesley. You each have a Pentium 600 computer with VGA monitor and laser color printer. We know you guys have had some experience in school with computers, and now you can cruise the net to your heart's desire. We love you, miss you, and are eagerly awaiting your return. Bob and Amy."

Round-eyed, with tears brimming, the boys gave each other the high-five.

"There must be a better word than awesome for this," stuttered Tommy. "Does everybody realize that we can travel all over the cyberspace highways?"

"It's uncanny, for sure. We can wander through data from the pyramids of Egypt, the ruins of ancient Rome, and to the hives of all the world's greatest cities. Boy, this surprise is almost as important as oxygen, right, Lane?"

"In today's fast-paced world, it would seem that way, Chad. But you have a job to do with your lab, too. How about teaching us old folks how to operate computers?"

"Piece of cake, Lane. That's a promise! Gee, Tommy, let's get back to the material we already have. We can fill up more than one disk for sure. For instance, we can make up cool question and answer games, like 'Where is the continental divide?' Who knows?"

Dead silence from the front seats. But Tommy frantically flipped through his notes.

"Just east of Butte, Montana. Now it's my turn. What is the motto on Montana license plates?"

"The Big Sky Country. And y'know what, the sky really does look bigger, 'cause everything is so flat."

This type of activity kept the whole group busy on the long trip home. At last they finally approached the Wellesley property, and even Nell and Millie were excited. They knew where they were. Tommy spied a red rocket-shaped car in their driveway. "Wow, look at those wheels. That must go from zero to seven million in thirty-five seconds. That's gotta be Bob's unless Chuck Yeager is visiting."

The Hamiltons were home.

Epilogue

Isn't there an old saying, "Out of adversity comes triumph"?

To this day, embedded in a massive boulder at the foot of Mt. McKinley, on the edge of a raging torrential creek, is a brass plaque which reads:

REX
1916–1986.

Its true legend is known only by Rex and the one woman whom he ever truly loved and trusted.